THE GREAT CIRCLE OF TIME

WILL PARFITT

I0589091

Will Parfitt has explored personal and spiritual development for more than forty years. Trained in Psychosynthesis and a Kabbalah teacher, Will lives in Glastonbury, England, where he offers mentoring, supervision and spiritual guidance.

Will can be contacted via his website: www.willparfitt.com

THE GREAT CIRCLE
OF TIME

WILL PARFITT

PS AVALON
Glastonbury, England

© Will Parfitt

First published in the U.K. in 2015 by PS Avalon

PS Avalon
BM Synthesis
London, WC1N 3XX, U.K.
www.willparfitt.com

Design: Will Parfitt

ISBN 978-0-9572246-5-0

"Experience is where the ideas come from. But a story isn't a mirror of what happened. Fiction is experience translated by, transformed by, transfigured by the imagination. Truth includes but is not coextensive with fact. Truth in art is not imitation, but reincarnation."
— *Ursula K. Le Guin*

"These walls could be my eyes where waking dreams unfold.
The air makes shapes, revolutions come and go,
One crack the escape every wind on earth howls through."
— *Susheela Raman*

ACKNOWLEDGEMENTS

The Ursula K. Le Guin quote is from *The Wave in the Mind*,
Shambala, Boston, 2004 [isbn 1-59030-006-8] page 268

The Susheela Raman quote is from the song *Magdalene*
on her album *Vel*, 2011. Publisher: Wardlaw Music.
Composers: Raman/Mills/Durvesh

July 23

Another glorious day as I sit and write this in the shade of a large copper beech tree in this beautiful garden. My journal is like my body with its sun-bleached cover and the blood in its veins. I'm an unfolding book, another page turns, and turns, and turns yet in this moment, I am all that I can be. This is my life, now.

Call me a fool to write then because words are not my favourite medium. I prefer actions. I could dance you my life right now, but to explain how I do it ... well. You should ask my brother the magician, he lives the same life but in a different way than me. His ways are about doing, doing this or that, doing life and death. My way is more about becoming something new in every moment.

My dance is a little dance, with many spirals contained within larger spirals and each containing many smaller ones. See, it would be easy to show you with a dance. Wheels within wheels. I just dance my life from one wheel to the next. It's my first and last dance, my only dance – I'm just making it last a while.

I forget how I got here. I know I've been here before and will be here again, same but different each time. That makes me laugh! Actually, of course, that's right – it's through forgetting that you develop – through forgetting the past events that have a hold on you. Not suppressing or repressing them, not making them shadow material through denying them, but simply yet fully and consciously and actively forgetting. It's as simple and as complex as that. You also need to forget the future. Forgetting that you have goals, forgetting you are going somewhere, doing something, and simply – complexly – allowing yourself to drift, to be on auto pilot, still on course, see, but not having to be in endless control.

You also need to learn how to forget the present. Yes, forgetting. There's too much emphasis placed on remembering – remembering yourself, remembering who you are, remembering your past lives, past traumas, and so on. Forget remembering! Remember to forget.

Indoors now, its early evening, and I'm languishing in the big arm chair. Pilgrim is somewhere nearby, and now I'm whispering to my journal as I enter:

My middle name is Innocence. I am the innocence of each moment, that's more like it. The innocence that is the moment between incarnations, the moment between being discarnate and coming into the waiting foetus, the moment between being still inside and being born, the moment between this and this – there's no 'that', this is my innocence.

Fool

You've made the choice to – whatever it is, anything – and you have moved into doing it, but it isn't done yet. The pie is cooking and you just don't know what it'll turn out like. Never mind you followed the recipe, or you made it up because you're a brilliantly intuitive cook, never mind you've made it a zillion times before and you know what it'll be like – prove it! You can't – and that's innocence. Take those moments and make them yours: flourish in them, embrace them, flaunt then, actively engage with them. They are the creative source, the innocence that is mistaken for childish and they are not. They are the children, the source of the offspring of your creativity.

It's said it is more important for you to have it rather than it having you. It's said. Whilst I agree with that, the problem is as soon as I agree with it, then something has got me. So I decide to agree with it and not agree with it at precisely the same time. I'm a clever sort of guy like that. So I also doggedly persist in holding my original conviction. Which of course I totally agree with!

You Fool!

I like the spring and early summer better than now. For me those times of year are sexual, everything growing with strength towards the sun, the blossoming of nature, the greening of the trees. The sap rises in spiralling cycles of energy. Enjoyed, loveable, loving spirals. Sometimes the sap doesn't seem to rise. Sometimes it feels stagnant or even as though it might be falling. Then a day comes when it rises again, thrusting up strong and throbbing with energy. We all know that feeling. That is my energy at all times, whenever, wherever (that's the deal, my dear.)

Passing through the moments when you are not talking to yourself, you almost catch a glimpse of me, but I am gone as soon as you see anything – so you think you must have imagined it. I was there. Tap me on the shoulder next time and remind me to be civil. I've a tongue in my head, as you've noticed. I can wish you good day and stay as easily as I can pass. You just make the space for me, and I'll be there.

I was born more than three minutes after my brother despite being conceived first, so it is more helpful to see me in the space between his birth and mine.

July 25

I am that I say I am.
I will be who I wish to be, what I wish to be, when and where I will.
And whatever will be will be.
So mote it be!

I am walking in a glade, a small clearing next to the path, with sun coming through the leaves, creating a pattern of dots with the leaves. My eyes are slightly blinded now by the light, but if I look in the opposite direction there is a mauve, purple glow. Pigeons are cooing in the distance. I am walking very gently and slowly so as not to disturb the deer. I'm coming into an opening where there's a tree on my left, bent over, creating an archway. There's an entrance through there into another world, with little golden creatures. I'm aware of a bright light just behind me. I can feel a tightening of my genitals and a shivery feeling.

I step over the edge, into an abyss of knowing and not-knowing.

July 26

Became not as-one, truly one.
I am a brother even if my brother is me. I am so attached to my little brother, more attached than he is to me, or than he has ever known. He will one day – soon, I believe. And what I wish will be, for I am a silent arrow that never misses its mark.

Magician

I really enjoy being in woods. I walk slowly, breathing the air slowly, treading lightly so as not to create a disturbance, yet I inevitably do. My will brings me forward, not forcing me but guiding me gently. I could curse the sound of the plane above, the machinery in the valley, if I were my shadow self. As my true self I lightly step forward through the undergrowth. I bless everything. I bless the sounds, the sights, the guardians and the place. As a magician I am concerned with my true will, my true will to walk the earth of this sacred land. I welcome my encounters with the beauty of nature – the light, the trees, the sky, the machinery. There is no difference.

I enjoy the sense of bringing power to earth, empowering the land, ensouling myself, ensouling the land, empowering myself. I walk silently, alone.

I step through gates that others do not see, and to worlds that others do see but do not understand.

I see a deer to the left of me. I pace forward silently. The deer looks, eyes wide and sees me seeing her. Deer, just turn and walk. Don't run. Have no fear.

I see a tiny beetle crawling across the ground, its black back sparkling in the light, reflecting the sky. At night the beetle reflects the god of midnight and the star goddess shining on its shiny surface.

Deer and beetle, birdsong and wind, what rare beauty, what common presence.

At that moment a tiny drop of dew fell from out of the tree and hit the first joint of my right thumb. Why did I notice it? I'm not here to answer the questions but to live the mystery.

The feather on the ground points forward.

I come out to the most beautiful clearing. A dry, open promontory, with grass growing in patterns on the dry mud, inviting me to sit down. To the south is a beautiful ash tree, growing into a double tree, ivy on it, so beautiful, split patterned leaves against the blue and white hazy sky. To the west is a single ash tree, with the sun, still high but on a downward path, shining through its wind-rustled leaves.

To the north is a single ash tree, one that breaks up into many smaller branches, each of which in turn breaks up into even smaller branches, reflecting the sun from the west, but also in harmony with the darkness approaching from the east. Standing resplendent in its imperfection, it is a mirror to the magician. All hail the place in the north.

In the east is a old, stunted ash tree, damaged at the top by acid rain, and yet so beautiful, I step towards it, knowing I have to touch it. With its stunted growth, bark peeled off, this tree marks a place where many come to connect. The tree of the east, so damaged, so hurt, and yet so very beautiful. I touch its bark. I feel a peaceful and yet vibrantly alive energy. And at that moment – listen, a cuckoo.

I now walk into the west, slipping forward into the twilight hours, descending down to a dark valley of tall trees. Like a jungle. Everything lives in here. I have to whisper.

Go down very slowly, blessed be.

A great vine hangs over the path, marking a passageway. I go down very slowly. As I come through the passageway, I can see the most incredible bird sitting on a branch to my right. It is a baby jay, really big and fluffy. It's got the jay's colouring and feathers. I don't know whether it can fly. Oh! Beautiful jay. Sammy Jay.

Ever so close to this bird now, I whisper: I could reach out and touch you. I love you. When we were children we had a friend called Sammy Jay who sometimes came in my dreams and sometimes came through our window. Me and my brother fed Sammy sweet cigarettes. My father knew all about it. Sammy Jay lives with me now. I'm focusing on this very young bird, relaxedly but with full attention. Hello. You are very beautiful but I wonder if you are safe there. What have you got to say?

Come with me into this world, just feel it for a moment.

With a note of sadness, an adult jay squawks in the tree above.

Over its multi-patterned, incredible beak, the young jay continues looking right at me with its beautiful big eye. We are less than a metre apart, face to face. I'm moving closer. Hi! I mean you no harm, and I am embarrassed to say some of us humans could, so be careful. You are so beautiful. That is your parent up there squawking for you, so I'll walk on not to cause you any problems. Live long and well.

I'm still in the deep, dark valley but now its breaking open and shafts of light are coming through. Bending down through an archway, I find the ground is strewn with heart-shaped light pink petals. There is a blackbird to my left, skipping, keeping its head down. I'm always seeing blackbirds ahead on the path, flying away. I protect blackbirds nests and curse the marauding magpie. And I worship the magic magpie. Six may be for gold but seven is a secret not to be told – not yet anyway. When you live within these riddles your magic too will flow –

Five riddles: the word; the vision; hearing the word; smelling the vision; tasting the earth.

Taste the earth, magician, and come through to the light where darkness dwells.

A spider's web breaks across my face. A thin gossamer strand tickling my third eye makes me ever so aware of a crack between the worlds. I take a step into another most beautiful clearing. Late sun shines on my face and warms my body. I strip off my clothes. I turn to the directions, letting each direction affect my body in its nakedness. The sap rises in the earth and in me. I worship father sun, shining on small blue, upright plants, their stalks covered with many small, strangely-shaped darkish-blue flowers with white stamens. White covered with the sexual energy, the energy of the sun that is the earth that is the mother-father in one.

I, magician, the child, step forward, through the last passage of darkness, into the birth canal from where I will step out. Yet at this moment, I feel trapped. Will I get through? I push my way, and shake my head as a twig spikes into my head. I can see a rabbit ahead and a magpie flies across my vision as I come through the canal, out into the joyous, laughing, vibrantly thrilling light.

There is a sound of drums, beating out a heavy rhythm. Something lands on my left eye, a strange creature with a beetle-black back. It turns into a piece of twig. A spider crawls away as I move down into the world of insects. I am here now. I am just aware of ash on the ground, white and grey fire ash.

I worship father sun, shining on this small blue planet.

July 30

I am born out of my brother at each moment. Sometimes I step back out of the moment into a space where I'm between moments. In those moments I am the magician, playing some role or other.

I am the magician now, writing for you about this. Stepping over into the space on the edge of the shadow and light, when I turn round, I find that the shadow has receded.

I pace down into the everyday world. Your world. And I find I'm looking into a copse where there are two women, one with black hair, one blond. Both very beautiful. Black haired woman is touching the blonde woman on the arm. She is wearing a light green tee-shirt and a dark green skirt. The blond woman is wearing patterns.

The dark woman reaches out to me, and I step forward into her arms. I don't know whether I am dreaming or being dreamed. It's all now. What's real and what isn't real? We magicians don't know, but can you be sure there are even magicians?

The blonde woman smiled. We are one, too, and free. Enter now.

Blessing and curses, they are not different.

July 31

She was wearing patterns of red and gold and green, the colours of a country of golden harvested fields. The patterns on her skirt looked like golden and green hay, stacked and left where it's been mown. With the red tee-shirt she looked the colour of a sunset. Containment at the end of the day. We kissed.

I had this sort of funky face on. Then I thought: where does that come from? Whose face am I imitating, with this funky expression? Then I thought, well I probably do a lot of

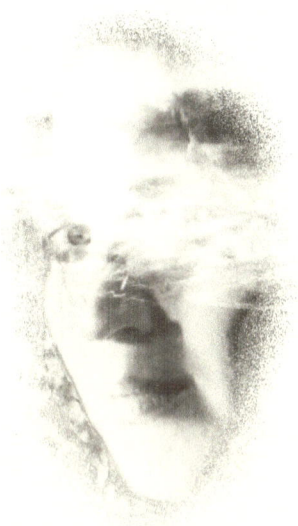

Priestess

impersonations, put on lots of masks that are other people's faces I'm imitating. All and everyone does that. You like a face, it attracts you, you see it at an important time in your life, you imitate it. Or you want to look groovy or cool or something particular. You develop your own faces, but they are part of all the repertoire of different masks.

I realised then that I can choose what face to put on. What face do I want? What is the most exciting face to imitate? The most important of all is to take the most beautiful smile in the world. I did it.

We laughed, she and I. My happiest, happiest face. I'll use it more and more and get more lines on my face, and I'll have happy lines rather than worried lines.

Pilgrim screeched with laughter. Then we can be bright together in our magic patchwork room.

There was a long silence.

There was a squeaking sound. Her eyes widened and her attention became sharp. It sounded like an inn sign, squeaking in the breeze. An in-sign?

I'll get my disguise, my don't-look-at-me-or-you-might-recognise-me face. We can mingle with the crowd.

August 1

Lughnasad. The beginning of the harvest for the world.

I can't just write here about my joy, I have to write of my pain too, for me to know it and for my brother to know it. This is the way of family, to share and share alike.

My therapy ended badly last week, and I am now going it alone.

Oh blessed Mary, let me come in you. I look into your eyes and I see heaven.

I came.

I can see your face so clearly, I whispered softly, strangely.

August 6

At the first gate Pilgrim noticed the two snakes that lay across her path so she raised her arms in the sign of the crescent moon. Swinging her arms, she walked carefree, carelessly stepping ahead. She touched her head, put both arms to her hair and bounced her curls. Artfully and aimlessly she walked the path, her swinging arms making a large Y as they stretched up to the air. The owl screeched as it flew from the tree in front of her. Disturbed, screeching but somehow also with her in her experience. She took a long stick from the ground, a small tree trunk that had broken off, and whipped it into the air. It span two times and landed. There! she exclaimed and started down the bank after the stick. At the spot where the end of the stick landed she knelt to the ground and eagerly dug her hands into the leaf strewn earth. She then draw a talisman from the soil.

It is nothing important, she said, just my life!

Pilgrim raised the talisman, put it to her lips and kissed it erotically. She placed it back and, with her fingers, scooped the earth into the hole, over the talisman. Standing, she stamped round a bit and carefully laid leaves over the place, making it look as if she hadn't been there. Then she carefully walked back up to the path, turned and waved to me. She knew I was watching. I walked towards her.

We were soon passing through the gate, she moving with a graceful, grateful step, me less so.

Things wind down at the end of the day. Out there is busy, but in here everything is winding down ready for the night. Responding to the sun. That is why we come here, we are responding to the sun, too. And it's new moon tonight. I looked up and she was delicately removing a spider's web from across her face, talking to it gently as she did so.

August 7

A pattern of feathers.

I am a shape switcher. I don't shift, I switch. I started this day as a small feather. One side of me was a feathery grey-brown colour. The other side had horizontal bands of grey, white, blue and black. Under the black was a really intense blue which faded slowly into lighter blue until it became white. I was a very beautiful feather.

In my earthly form today I take the form of this woman who although incarnated into a male body is nevertheless truly female and male, not combined but entwined and intertwined. Wind me up, wind me down, wind me round your little finger. Round me up, wound me down, wind me out, wind me in like a holy fisherman with a rod, and on the line the fish, the soft luscious juicy fish, which slides down the throats of men and women as they slip into earthy lust.

Fishing for time with a wishing line.

What wondrous place is this, this earth. The soles of my naked feet feel every atom of every mote on the face of the earth, and yet tread so softly they do not touch except barely to support my lightweight form. As I approach the great circle of time, I prepare to sing. My lovers, the trees are here. To sing, to break through the veil and enter the holy grove. How my lovers stand tall. They have roots which embrace my roots, they have trunks as firm as my desire, they have branches as many as my loves, they have a pattern as natural as my Love. On their branches are many leaves. Each leaf, embracing the air, sings silently of the same joy as I feel in my heart.

I am also the priestess of fear. I am the kind of fear you feel when on an edge: the kind of fear that borders excitement. Go to a secluded woods and take your clothes off. Naked under a tree, in a place where no one appears to be and yet someone might well come. The throbbing you feel is the blood in my arteries, is my excitement, throbbing through you. My fresh blood running through your arteries, is blue and red and yellow and white. It is blue like the night sky, a royal blue blood. The red is that of a living heart. The yellow is like the shining sun. The white is my own body, the moon.

I am always followed by my shadow, dark grey by day, ghostly white by night. I prefer depths, dark secret caves and alleyways, walkways and byways, and walking under the trees into the holy grove.

My body becomes an electric quiver of upright hair.

I become the most beautiful butterfly: dark slate grey, with a bright pink border, then as I fly all you see is a florescent pink flash across your green world. This world, to me now, is like a tropical forest. I fly to the tallest trees that reach out of the thick dense, entwining life of the undergrowth, reaching up to the sky. I float up to where a few branches suddenly burst out above the canopy and spread in a blaze of green spikes. I rest there, alone.

I am facing a beautiful cat.

Am I to pass, guardian of this place, or stay between forever?

I won't be leaving here until the holes of my decay widen. I am riddled with worms, moss has already eaten most of my right eye. Decay takes off most of my surface, and moulds and other parasitic creatures come and take of me until I am no more. Then when I am no more I will also be myself again.

You can pass.

I feel a great sense of relief, feel my breathing, as I am passing through.

My purpose for being here is to incarnate in and out of your body. When you breathe the sweet smell of summer into your nostrils, you are intimate with my secret scent. When you fill your lungs with the warm breeze of midsummer moon, you embrace the body of my known scent. Combine these two and you will be you.

From where I sit in the heavens the stars are like little deep purple pink flowers in a meadow of many rich green grasses. What you call a civilization I see as a bee sucking the honey from a flower and passing on the pollen to another.

My legs quiver with excitement as they part for the entrance, as they part for my lover, my dark sister.

I am Pilgrim now, opening for my man and opening for myself. Coiled.

August 9

Now I am charged with both the revealing and the concealing for the broken chain is my gift and my curse.

August 10

Today just is.

August 12

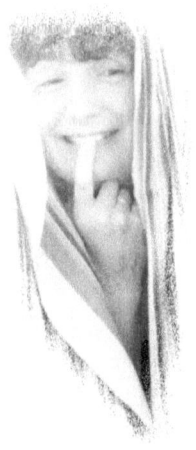

Empress

I am a sorceress. Where the priestess shape-switches, in me there is a permanence. People see me in different ways, but my permanence is exalted above all. I remind you of your need to stay connected and I remind you of your need to let go. I also remind you that at essence they are one thing.

Come into my body, said the most beautiful white faced goddess with purple lips and brown eyes. Come into my body and hear the birds sing. Tread the path that leads to my depths.

Around my permanence, my place, position and pole, revolve endless forms: flies buzzing, deer skipping, flowers growing. These endless forms are in constant states of decay whilst I remain.

If they see me, they are reminded of their passing. That is my curse. Those connected to wisdom, in passing, realise their permanence. That is my blessing.

When you approach me you bend low three times, when all I ask is one kiss.

Houses decay, the air is passing, the air is passing, houses decay. Camels may ride the desert, but it is only I who opens the door.

Bend down again brother, rise up lover. Who can distinguish the lover from the brother, or the father from the sister, or the uncle from the aunt, is a maker of humans.

This is the most beautiful place, the place in which I dwell. There is the water here which I gulp down as soon as it touches my lips. The birds sing. Splendour on the earth is my secret name. There is absolutely no longing in the heart, simply belonging.

The elixir of life on my lips, a gentle melodious swing to my hips, I step over the dead and dying. Rise up from my heart like a silver and maroon bird in flight. Rise up to the treetop. I touch the tree, and – hah, my heart leaps.

Oh, bend low once more and bend again. Bend thrice and the sorceress is with you. Put your hands on me, mortal. Feel my hips, my lips. You can hear the sound of my heavy breathing.

I am the perfection of love and will, the horizontal arm of the cross. My arms open, emphasizing my eternal embrace. How can I fail? I reach the very roots of the tree. I am breathing and smiling, as I take my breath. The roots of the tree.

Deafeningly, the bird song is reflected here.

August 23

If I hadn't been here before, would I notice the signposts? In the woods I find the sorceress in a million forms of little creatures, all teasing one another, and me, with little games of touch and dare. Little fly, bird, and the black butterfly, all wing past my eyes, with a chuckle.

My sign is a fist with the thumb pointing to the right. There is a feather on the ground underneath the fist.

Freed from carrying the stick, I put the water to my lips and drink. This is a time for life, for breathing freely. The sun is going down from between the clouds, after rain, and the air is so clear, the light so bright. As I turn around me, I see the most beautiful yellow flowers, brightly lit in the sunshine, glowing under the grey clouds.

My body is beautiful, my body is as delicate and sweet as a butterfly, and strong as the earth of which it is made. My body smells sweetly. I am full of great laughter. I take a deep breath and the air is sweet. I am exalted and I am the earth, energised. Simply look, stop and look.

Growing out of the closed-up, five-sided pods, when they open, is a star of sepals that surround a circle of pink and mauve flowers. Crawling onto one of those flowers now is a small flying beetle with the most beautiful orangey-red back. She is exquisite. Now I see a smaller beetle, very small, climbing onto the top of the flower, struggling to get there. Then it is putting its tongue deep into the honey, whilst on its back, its mate is copulating.

At the sound of a bumble bee passing we all stop.

I suck the honey at both ends, I ride on the back of my lover. She: my lover rides on my back. As I suck the sweet nectar from between the stamens of the bright yellow sun, amidst the buzzing of insects, I enter paradise, here today.

I am ready to walk back home. I put my spell on you, beautiful land, that you put your spell on me. I walk this earth as a guardian of sacred places. And I step away.

August 24

I am a sorceress. I am beautiful in every way. I am two round hills and the valley between that leads down to the healing waters. I am all of this. I am a sorceress. I am Pilgrim.

I am the land, I am your mother and your devourer. Despite my great age, I am still young. It is sunny. I sit in a very beautiful, dull-green bowl with an orange brim, out of which bursts a mass of foliage. Oval shaped deep green leaves hang downwards from my upright stem. I am surrounded by clusters of beautiful bright purple flowers, ranging from deep dark purple, in which the shadows are black, to very much lighter purple in which the shadows are almost ice white. The relationship between you and me is symbiotic and totally conscious. Any lack of consciousness is on my part. How do you stay in touch with me, here where the plants glow with light energy?

August 27

There is a backstory that illuminates the now, always. Mrs Roach was on the ground floor and we had the two floors above. From the top floor window you could look at part of a cricket pitch in the pavilion opposite. I recall seeing a cricket match. Then I realise it was in that house, where we only lived for nine months at the most, when I was five, when I first started school, that my father told me a secret. A pivotal time in my life. Lots of things happened in that nine months. It's where I lost my eyesight – when my eyes took on short-sightedness, it cancelled memories of so many different things at once.

August 31

I resisted him as he struck out at me, the side of my head feeling the full force of his backhand. We were both in the bathroom at the time. The tiles lit up as I fell backwards, stumbled, then crumpled against the wall behind. I saw stars, maybe a dozen or so different coloured stars, larger than the largest stars in the sky, but only just, and twinklingly bright. Amidst the emotional and physical pain my consciousness moved to the excitement of seeing stars – really seeing them! I'd seen it in comics but I'd never guessed it was literal. Thanks, for the stars, and no thanks for the scars.

September 5

I held the emotional pain quietly in the depths of my muscle and bone. I filed away the mental pain in a folder marked forget. The physical pain I coped with, and the emotional pain only added to what I already felt in that area. As for the worst pain, the spiritual pain, I took it on, past all the ancestors back to the first human. Then I started to learn how to deal with it in my way. I was determined not to deal with it my ancestor's way, even then.

I no longer have to deal with that pain for my allies protect me. I have remembered it and cleared its hold on my body. I play my parts now with choice. My parts are released. My ancestors are dead and their parts have been consummated in fire, water, air and earth and released for their journey.

September 8

I stepped through a gate and walked up a gently sloping lawn towards a group of three men, sitting on seats that looked rather

Emperor

too sumptuous to be outdoors. To my left I saw a large building. It looked like a palace. The seats were certainly palatial, and as I walked closer I could see that one of the men was a king, or a sultan, or – I guessed – an emperor who lived in the palace. The way he was dressed suggested it, but the way he held court over the other two men said it all.

Sitting on the grass between the supposed emperor and his two henchmen, I joined in their conversation. I asked the emperor what he was talking about. He stopped talking and looked rather shocked to be interrupted. I just smiled at him.

September 9

Listen even if this upsets you, remember:

I am considerate in the true meaning of the word.

The world revolves around me. When I move anywhere the world follows along, always keeping me at the centre. I am a point at the middle of a circle.

Wherever you move you remain the centre of the circle. Imagine you are standing somewhere on a vast open plain that reaches as far as you can see in every direction. You can see the horizon ahead, and it is curved. You turn around, keeping your attention on the horizon and you can see you are standing at the centre of a circle. Now take a few steps in any direction and do it again. See! You are still at the centre.

As I sat facing the sun, the light penetrated the different coloured petals on the flowers, making them translucent. Only the edges of the large orange daisy were lit in this way. The centre was a deep, velvety textured orange that let through the light. On one edge of the flower stood a butterfly, wings being flapped around by the wind. Its colours caught the sunlight and flashed.

We fill our circles up with buildings, trees, flowers, people, cities, palaces, grass, butterflies – and that's just the outer stuff. We also fill our circles with lots of different emotions tied up with one another in endless lengths of multicoloured twine – some of it barbed, some of it with a sting, some the most beautiful colours that instantly raise joy in the heart. All entwined. And then all those thoughts we put into our circles – constructive ones and destructive ones, ones that create new worlds, or re-create old worlds, ones that destroy worlds, and people, and plants, and everything else we put in our circles. All the fantasies, lies, illusions.

I feel sad, deeply sad.

Words are not enough and even when they are, they only convey what we know inside already. Lift up your heart, those are words too, and ones that bring cheer.

I am the emperor. I sit at the centre of my circle whatever is going on around me. Sometimes I let the universe within my circle change and evolve as it will. Sometimes I use my will – like what? How?

Like a silent, invisible player in a game of cosmic cricket.

And I create and change and cause things to happen in my circle. Look – at my command the butterfly moves on to another flower.

And the sun comes from behind that haze, and brightens.

The flower shone vibrantly round the edges whilst the dense deep orange centre seemed to reflect the purples, pinks, and blues of the flowers behind, creating a psychedelic kaleidoscope of colour.

Then the sun went behind a cloud. That's not my fault!

I stretched out my left arm, finger pointing to the cloud that was passing over the sun. An emperor butterfly came and alighted on my finger. The wind blew its wings, and it looked like it had to cling on as tightly as it could not to be blown away. The more the wind gusted, the more the butterfly clung to my finger. I felt mesmerised by its strength, its beauty, its life.

The wind stilled and the sun came again momentarily. I started shaking my left hand to dislodge the butterfly with a gentleness that sharply contrasted with the wind's strength. The world is always mystery, a wonderful mystery.

I stood and watched as the emperor and his two old friends strolled up the lawn towards the palace buildings. They laughed boisterously and one of them started to sing the words of a bawdy song. I couldn't tell which of them was singing, but soon it didn't matter for the other two joined in. Smiling contentedly, I glanced at the sun and, turning to my left, stepped back through the gate.

September 21

The equinox at last, now we can go deeply into autumn with all the colourful pain of dying leaves that brings. Hail the turning of the year. The world of sorrow and joy.

Walking in the woods on your own requires the courage to be very small. Then you step over snakes, and laugh with wild dogs as they pass. Walking in the woods requires the silence of the rabbit and the stealth of the cat, then the magician's wand laid across your path means nothing. You hear the deer before they hear you.

You sense the presence of others before they can run for cover.

In the dense jungle of life, the walking is forever. I know for I am a priest. I take no action of my own. Thy will is my will. I am a priest without a hierarchy. I do not reside at the centre, you always find me at the periphery. When I move to the centre, I do so with caution, watching for red berries to mark my way. Swing low sweet chariot, the body of bliss.

Priest

So many flies owe their existence to my excrement. I open the door and they enter. What is my life, what is their life, but the passing of moments?

Our laughter echoes through the aeons, whilst I walk like a man through the undergrowth of the earth forest. Red berries guide me where to go as I pass. The sun is so bright I scatter my clothes to the wind, to the breeze. My naked body is beclothed in a raiment of light, from the purple ground of my feet to the shining light within.

I turn to face my brother and he is already gone. He is no more. Where he dropped his stick, I bless the place, with my step, my bow, my hand on the earth, my rising and my letting go. Blessings be!

My task is the counting of days. As each day is the same, my task is difficult, so I step across the worlds and walk into your time. I am bitten and bruised by the journey, but the sun is healing.

It is so beautiful here, I just walk. What is there to say when you walk in beauty? Silent words from my heart drop at my feet.

September 30

The woman from the human tribe is truly blessed. The birds sing a sweet song of blessings. My breath is in harmony with theirs, as theirs is with hers.

A beautiful pink flower has dropped from the bouquet. It has five bright, light-pink petals, several flowers on a small stem, with minute little stamens rising from the centre, tipped with yellow.

Two thistles, with just a splash of purple around the edges of their silver faces, sway as I pass. This is the most beautiful meadow.

This has been experienced before; it will be experienced again; it is only experienced now.

Rise up to life, my dear other, and allow yourself to feel the power of the priest within your bones and your flesh, your sinews and your heart, within your loins, within your earth.

This is paradise.

I am the priest and I intone a banishing ritual. Begone foul people who pollute the land. Begone with your horrible bits of rubbish, with your paper and your tins, with this piece of bent wire that I trod upon. Begone you foul people, begone from this place and never come back. I am taking this piece of metal, bent into a strange shape, and with it goes a curse upon you if you come back to this place with pollution. If you will, come back and enjoy, and be with it, and take your rubbish away. If you don't, may you be cursed unto the ages.

When the priest meets other people, he is timid and shy. Only the true notice him, for those with faults unto themselves can only see the faults in others. This is the truth the priest speaks. I am the priest. There is no need for any other truth. I have absorbed the other and we now are one. Our purpose is to walk the earth of this blessed place, this paradise. We breathe the warm air deep into our lungs then we are reminded of the near future, the now.

I step into each now. I feel the now I step out of, behind me. It recedes fast and once again I am on my own.

October 2

I am not a gardener, I am a friend of the garden. The garden is my friend, and we meet, whatever our moods. Sometimes I hardly notice my friend yet I am still in deep relationship with her. We spark off each other, not always in the most comfortable of ways, but always in the most honest, real way. She has no edge, and I aspire to her centre, her heart. All around me, yet she is also within my heart, held in my centre in a constant act of perfect friendship. Even when I fail – which is often – she still holds me, embraces me with her trust. For this, we meet as lovers in the moments when our bodies call. I tend the soil of her body; I nurture and support her whilst she sustains and feeds me.

I'll write later about what I found there, it is too secret to write yet.

October 4

I'm smiling now. We do have a biofeedback aspect to us, don't we? Like if I consciously start to choose to think about smiling, you know, I don't mean forcing one, I mean, there are always things to smile about if you connect with it. Like right now. I can purposely put on a smile, in a sense, or focus on something to smile about, and its like smile and the whole world smiles with you. That's a cliché but true.

October 7

I felt disturbed about putting kittens in the oven.
      Like putting a bun in your oven.

October 8

It's not the ego that wants money. It's the soul that wants money. The soul wants time like this, more time like this. The soul likes coming to places like this and hanging out.

If it's soul wants money in order to get time to hang out, then is it a more pure desire than if it was an ego desire? That's how it happens, the fool still lives within every hue.

We live in paradise.

And then we get caught in doing it our way rather than thy way.

Yes, like let thy will rather than my will be done.

It happens then. We are surrounded by abundance. That's how you find happiness with whatever you've got. Because there is always perfection. It's paradise. I forget it quite often but its true.

What happened to the end of my finger? There's blood.

When I came through the gate, I almost lost a few molecules. I got the molecules back but there was a seepage of blood, yes.

October 9

Eris's day.

All hail Eris-Pilgrim, the luscious queen of sight and sound. She rides upon me with her bright pink body. I raise my seven heads, my seven heads rise to her splendour. My body loves…

Earlier today, I heard a voice, he said: I am your first. I distinctly heard the man's voice right within my head. Somewhere just behind my eyes there was a slight pain.

Lovers

I noticed my brother was becoming agitated. We hadn't seen each other for a while.

And the sixth, in whose centre is the heaven at seven, is an image: being ridden by the beautiful woman-goddess, his energy, his penis pulsing, her spine, her spine, her body pulsing around her spine, the vein up the middle, as his penis she throbs. When he comes her head explodes and they are united, beauty and the beast. And everything relaxes in the abyss of co-created bliss.

And my brother could never understand a word of this, so long as they deny his existence, then he doesn't even seem to remember, well, how can I tell him? Can I share with him who he really is?

October 18

Lindy was my first real girlfriend. We were sixteen. She was mad for life. She was drunk. She was exhilarating. I ran after her. Whenever I looked up her skirt, I could see she wasn't wearing knickers. Never did.

It was Lindy first told me about the children of the dragon flame. It was as I entered her as we lay on the centre of a small busy roundabout in the centre of a fairly busy road. Listen, I remember you Lindy, I remember your white inner thighs, your flesh, your steaming jewel! Maybe I will show this journal to you one day and I will see up your skirt again!

We are the children of the dragon flame. We are bright and light, and we dance our dreams into a crazy nakedness. We are focusing our energy on our genitals and allowing the sensuality of that energy to permeate and flow through our bodies, and into our lungs and we breathe out our sensuousness into our aura. We are sensitive to all sexual things so we glow. All around there is nothing but sexual things, like a living stream in which the children of the dragon flame swim. As the children of this energy we are constantly merging and separating, moving from oneness into duality and back again in a waxing and waning flow of form.

October 19

The whole room became like a blue bubble in which Lindy and I sat. The light had a crystal quality to it which reflected in Lindy's blue eyes. She smiled at me so sweetly I felt all the hairs on my body flip into action and stand. Something was going to happen.

My lips moved towards hers and met with an electric smash. Instantly her tongue pushed into my mouth, wet and warm, causing my penis to swell rapidly. Our mouths kissed and it was all that existed, the kiss. Her tongue was probing deeply into my mouth and I was sort of chewing it. Chewing it! Pulling back I saw, as her face came into vision, that she was smiling. Blood was pouring out of her mouth, and she was dribbling little pieces of her chewed tongue. Have me, she said. Have me now. We are the children of the dragon flame.

We are the children of the dragon flame. We wear clothes that flaunt our sensual bodies, for we are out for sex, any chance we get. We don't always act it out, sometimes we spend many years, centuries, allowing ourselves to sink into a reverie of passionate longing. Only so that when we let go of that waiting our pleasure is intensified. We are always juicy, and if we are not, we will be so at a touch. We are lovers of the excess of life, living for the merging with goddess consciousness. We are flowing with the tide of energy at the level that pleasures us most. We are children, not slaves, and our parents adore us. They give us their all. We consume them utterly.

October 20

The man was level with us. We carried on pretending to talk but watched him closely as he slowed almost to a stop. He probably couldn't believe his eyes. With her skirt raised right up, and no knickers, her genitals on full view, her labia pink and puffy amidst her light brown pubic hair. The air was charged with electricity. I noticed he had a hand in one pocket and was clearly rubbing himself hard. Lindy turned to look at him and smiled her best come-on, at the same time parting her legs wider, causing the flesh on her thighs to wobble. The man rushed off, it was clearly too much for him.

Of course, Lindy wanted me to have her right away, right then. I did!

We are the children of the dragon flame. We step into the sunshine for we love to bask in the light, our bodies naked thrilling in the warmth and sensuality of life. We love life. We are vain and narcissistic and we pride ourselves on the spiritual strength we gain from our uncompromising stance. We feed on the freedom to be ourselves. We do not strive after perfection when we live our lives perfectly.

October 21

Safe sex is in the magic of inspiration, the touch of imagination and the tongue of initiation. Come in the way of eyes, see even the invisible line of our beautiful forms. Come in the way of ears, resonate to the joyous vibration of our tuneful laughter. Come in ways of deep scents, entrap us in a single flower, a glorious harmony of musk.

Come in ways of tastes, burn our breath yet succour and sweeten our tongues with the delight of almonds and the glory of pure liquid, from springs and fountains that flow freely from mother. Come in ways of touching, not holding back from touching with fingertips the warm blood of earth or grasping with palms the cold waters of the stars.

October 22

Tonight was the inauguration of a meeting of the children of the dragon flame. The platform speaker was introducing the opening session. Once every eleven years we, the children of the dragon flame, are brought together for a meeting to discuss the state of the world from our perspective and to generally tune in to the collective sexual energy our combined presence can generate.

All the participants were obviously energised, speaking fast and freely, half an ear on the speaker, their attention mostly on their neighbours' conversations. It took me a little while to orient myself to their voices, they seemed to come so fast. I was also stunned by the mass of naked flesh before me.

I made notes through the meeting of what various people said.

Where there is ecstasy, there is creation.

The word made flesh.

Knowledge of the flame opens the gates into other worlds.

Breath is life.

There is a bridge between time and eternity.

There is a snake coiled three times, that ascends to the seven through the perfect fifth and the united sixth. It ascends to the seventh. The four petals are the foreplay for the height of the eight at her heart.

Some mouths were in contact sealing each other. They looked straight into each others' eyes, and energies were exchanged not lost. Seal the nose and close the ears, too. Create the mystic seal, seven fold.

The mushroom flourishes between her moist lips, between the legs of the goddess. She is beautiful, the goddess, the eight petals at her heart drop nectar into the sun at her rounded belly, where it is consumed by the fire and then drips invisibly into the crescent moon, from where we drink.

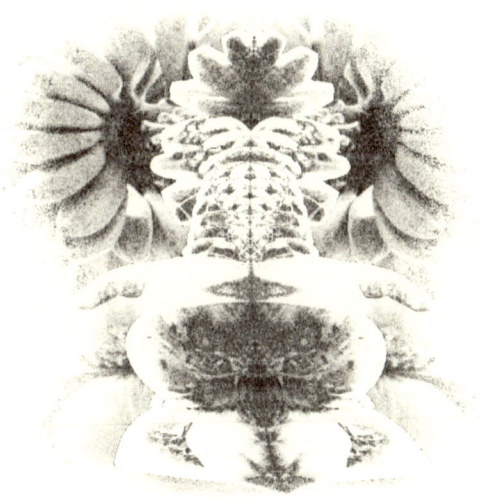

Chariot

Watch the third attention slip through your fingers and toes. Enter the cave of ecstasy.

Heaven expands, earth contracts, a rich fruity olive flavour with a spicy back note.

Cosmic fire and cosmic water in union.

I was making love yesterday evening to a young woman I hooked up with, she reminded me of Lindy.

There was the sound of a shakuhachi playing wistfully yet exotically in the background whilst our lips alternately met and parted. Wrapping the fingers of her left hand around my erect penis, just below the glans, she squeezed gently. With her other hand she stroked my left nipple. She gazed back into my eyes.

It seemed like we were making love in a rose filled garden even though we were indoors, in my bedroom. Not only that, each thorn had been carefully removed from each rose stem, of which there were seemingly millions.

Many years before, with the help of my brother, I had chosen her from amongst the women, and carried her to the centre of the circular garden. She squealed with delight as I placed her on the earth at the centre of the circle, and slid her skirt up over her thighs. Her legs parted and the world span. There was a flame between her eyes.

She spread her legs as wide as she could. There was that look in her eyes as her vaginal juices dribbled and ran down the pulsing vein which stretches along the back of my penis.

Our blending constituted the first link in the sequence of the elements.

Her hips pulsed as she deeply impaled herself.

This is spirit, this is soul, this is shadow, we are one. Her sweet lips tenderly spoke these words just before merging with my lips.

The voices of the children were louder than ever. Multicoloured statements formed, almost like playing blocks, above them.

The superiority of a person is not obvious to the eye but lies hidden within, from view. He who comes out in the world can no longer be contained.

Truth did not come into the world naked but in images then words. One will not experience truth in any other way.

We concentrate on the concrete experience rather than the abstract principle. How could it be there is neither a summer nor winter if you feel hot in summer and cold in winter?

In action there is no labour, in non action there is illumination.

Seeming to rise above the ground and float, yet still writhing together, the naked bodies of our entwined selves created the most beautiful word pictures yet.

Yesterday I planted an aubergine, today the winter melon.

But she spreads, and demands more room alive than dead, and now the summoned fishers moist.

All beasts that move on the earth, all the fish of the sea and fowl of the air are given to your power. You should eat figs, tasting the juice of thine angel.

With the goddess absent, dead leaves are piling and all is deserted.

This receiving is a not receiving, thou art my lover, I see thee as a nymph with her white limbs stretched by the spring.

Oak of god in thy branches in the lightening nested, above thee hangs the eyeless hawk.

The full moon, only lovely, flawlessly clear.

For the pine tree, see how green it is. I am here. My hermitage is thatched with morning glory.

In the midst of all this, a great and high altar formed. Angels beyond count, thousands and thousands, ten thousand times ten thousand angels were circling this altar.

I was again hearing the words spoken by the platform speaker, forming clearly in my mind, words I partly recognized. Congealed on earth, but does dissolving run into the glories of the almighty sun.

You do not understand the words of life because you are in death. Darkness darkens your eyes and your ears are stopped with deafness.

I will kiss you and bring you to the bridal. I will spread a feast before you in the house of happiness, I am not come to rebuke or enslave you, I bid you not turn from your voluptuous ways, your follies. All you do is right if you enjoy it.

I was thrilled by these words, spoken so softly and lovingly. For a moment I didn't notice that the platform speaker, all the children of the dragon flame – everyone had stopped what they were doing and were staring at me as they expected me to speak.

There was an ancient town called Good-To-Live-In. A mighty king called there one day and couldn't understand why it was called Good-To-Live-In. To him it looked like a hovel. He summoned the wisest man in the town and demanded to know why it was called Good-To-Live-In.

The wise man looked gently into the king's eyes and replied. When you realize this place is neither good to live in nor bad to live in, then you will realise it is Good-To-Live-In.

October 24

It was no chance that I bumped into Lindy yesterday. Both shopping in London, both happening to be in Camden at the same time. Of course I went to have tea with her. It was exciting to see her again after so long

I was thrilled she remembered how long it had been. Eleven years.

She told me I'd been a good teacher to her. I felt embarrassed and told her she had been a good teacher too. I was also embarrassed when I thought what she had taught me, but delighted to remember.

She looked at me over and over with a touch of her come-on look in her eyes. Then, to my amazement, she suggested we could rent a room for a couple of hours that afternoon.

Then she showed me something. She crossed her legs slowly. I saw she still didn't wear knickers.

We are the children of the dragon flame still, she said. I wanted to, but I couldn't. It was so exciting. But I muffed it.

Should I have, dear diary? I wish I had now, her luscious lips. Am I stupid or just sick – or just honest to a deeper conscience that knows my soul's deepest wishes?

November 14

Strength

A long time since I wrote here. Let me tell you what happened. I need to write it down to try and steady myself. As I came out of the gate, I found myself lying on the floor. I stood and started walking, feeling slightly wobbly, very excited to be in this new world. It was very bright and the beauty of the place was astounding. There was one, very earth-like sun. Leaves, brightly coloured, unnaturally bright, were strewn on the path.

I could see Pilgrim, walking ahead slowly. Maybe she is waiting for me to catch her up. No, she is moving faster again now. I love Pilgrim being here – she isn't everywhere but I meet her so often. To have a female soul who travels as I do is such a bonus.

There was a strange smell in the air – a sort of mentholated green smell with a slightly acrid under-edge. I rushed ahead to catch up with Pilgrim.

She turned and greeted me. She told me that if you stay static, you limit yourself. We have a wide range of things to go for. You might never go to the same place again or it might have changed when you return, so make the most of it now.

I was pointing to our left and something metal partly hidden in the bushes. We walked over in amazement.

It looked like a spaceship had landed there, and embedded itself in the earth, just this metal hull sticking out. Could it have been that? It sure looked like it.

Well, it could be spaceships, angels, natural power sources, who knows – sow the seed – the power is common to everywhere. Sometimes we overlay it with things that make it more or less accessible.

And also our other activities affect it. For instance, if it is a place where nature is treated kindly, then the power is more accessible than at a place where humans misuse the power.

Well, what could we do but walk on eventually. Should we tell someone. It was too much like the x-files and anyway, others must have seen it already. The rational mind does that, moves you on. We couldn't know who to tell in this world anyway.

Pilgrim told me how she walks in all the worlds. You make sure your toes are spread out, contacting the ground at each footfall. And then you slightly shake your ankles as they come up and down to help them relax. You bring your attention up to your pelvis and tilt it forward slightly. Then you come to the shoulders. You bring them back a bit and you stretch up your spine and pull up from the crown.

Pilgrim and I walked down into a ravine, marveling at the shapes we could discern in the broken rock face of the ravine.

Pilgrim told me that, eight hundred years ago, she had came to this ravine, making a triangle with her body and lying in an ancient vagina shaped cave hidden deep in the ravine. She said she was afraid of lots of spiders coming into her, but not afraid of the fish, the soft luscious juicy fish, sliding down her throat, deep in the ravine revealed.

She smiled as she remembered how she had catharted her pain those hundreds of years ago.

I told her I'm glad she is not fearful of spiders now.

We didn't find the cave but I found her cave and entered it. In the open, in the sunshine.

November 18

There's no me left to write anything here, I don't go out, I do go in, I don't go up and I do go down.

November 25

The energy was used, and we turned to the nearest gate to return to our own time.

In this world, I noted to myself, there are creatures that look like mushrooms. They wear pointed hats and are tall and thin. They look like the mushroom you find between the labia of every woman.

Just before passing through the gate, I dropped to my knees in wonderment. The seed is everywhere.

December 21

Hermit

The solstice story begins, the pageant of entering the underworld and disappearing for three days before rising again as a baby from the womb of a Mary or a mary, which one? Mary marry mary me!

Before me there were the moss-covered steps leading up to the outer ramparts of an ancient ruined city. The wind was howling. I closely kept my attention on a strange-looking dog who was staring at me. The gate opened and the dog disappeared.

Strange vibrations, sounding like airplanes, came out of the walls of an archway as I stepped through into this different world. A world made of patchwork silk, each piece of the patchwork, each patch, a different shade of gold. This whole world sparkled as the sun shined on the quilt. I felt illustrious. Stepping over a crack that looked very deep, I slowed down as the sun beat strongly on my naked body. The hermit, the secret seed, was dancing in my loins.

We are illustrious, we walk the land, softly treading, not bending the grass, not squashing the leaves, each step a step forward, we walk.

We clambered down to an ancient spring. A solitary bird was calling. My ears were filled with the sound of the dripping water and of a dog's barking background.

In the first shallow pool made by the spring, an old man was crouching besides the water. He had thick, snowy-white eyebrows and a full white beard. He looked so strong as he slowly slid into the water, right under it, and into dreaming. At that same instant, a white dove appeared to the left of the stream. The light brightened. I turned my head to the left and looked up at the white dove.

The bird communicated to me, said it was the emblem of the secret seed, the totem of the hermit. Then the dove somehow changed into a large crocodile type creature, but with wings. The secret seed, the blending of love and will, it said.

I realised what the bird/crocodile meant. The hermit and the lovers united become the man of earth, the time traveller, me.

I walked forward into the space beside the creature, stepping slowly and gently, seeing it continuously shifting between a white dove and a crocodile.

I could see love. Brushing spider webs from my hair, I walked towards the body of the crocodile. I was sharply pulled up by the energy. Emblazoned in the energy radiating from the near-side of the creature were the letters: mgn. Somehow I knew this translated as the secret seed.

I walked up towards the body of the being, encircled its trunk with my arm and then turned to face its bright green face. Face to face.

I could read the consciousness of this being. Its body was full of the heavens. It seemed to laugh eternally as life rushed through it. A truly holy being.

I heard amazing, flashing, alien voices. I stood mesmerized as a silent flying snake hovered before my face, flashing its shadow across the sun. The snake lurched at me, right at the left of my vision. Stepping forward I took the snake in my hand and pulled it to the ground.

Now when I put my fingers into my ears the sounds of the aliens are still there.

Looking down, I saw at my feet a purple and golden rod about one and a half metres long. I had a dim memory of a wand left somewhere by a magician. I picked it up and it felt like it had been designed for my use as a staff for the final ascent towards the summit of this sharp sloping peak.

At the top, it was very tight, entering the inner sanctum of the secret seed. What a wholly beautifully place it was, though. A place filled with love. The place of love itself.

Pilgrim and I went thrice in the holy water of the sacred well, thrice again, thrice again, and with three steps forward, through the gate. A choir sang.

I had filled my water bottle at the spring. Now I drank from it. Whilst I drank from the bottle I rested my new staff against my solar plexus. When I picked it up, it had changed in quality again.

The secret seed is already united through the hermit's communing The secret seed is manifest in the breath of the hermit.

Here we go, a descent into a cave, just into the opening of the cave, now slightly damp with anticipation, very silently moving forward so as not to disturb any creatures that might be here.

The wind was rushing through the edge of the cave. In the vestibule, a large cavern-shaped opening, lots of bats and birds were milling about. They came in and out of lots of entrances into smaller caves.

One of the entrances was shut, and attracted my attention. There was a bar next to the entrance with a spiral shaped twist in it. I reached forward and slipped my hands around the twist, to try turning the bar. Nervously, heavily and yet with confidence, I exerted force. The bar turned and a gate opened. I thanked the guardian of this gate and stepped through, bowing slightly as I did so.

I stood face to face with my brother. Each world is composed of many worlds, I told him. In each world there are eleven worlds and in each of those eleven worlds, eleven worlds more, and so on. We, of course, are also one of eleven worlds in a bigger world in which we live ... which is then also part of a bigger world. That's nothing new, you know it all. But you seem to need reminding.

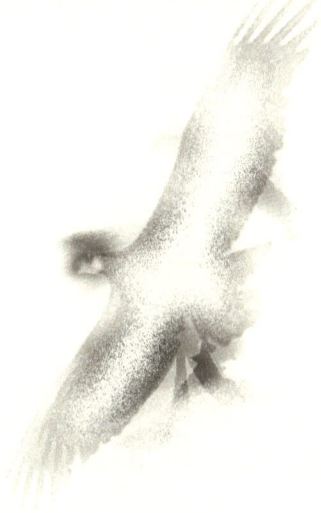

Fortune

I'm talking to my brother, my dumb brother, who is the hermit. The secret seed has united with the land. Blessings in joy of the land.

I lifted the bottle of holy spring water to my lips and drank.

He asked me to let him drink of that holy water in my bottle.

I banged my staff against a nearby post.

He rubbed his finger nails together making a sound like a washboard in a skiffle band.

Ha! we bellowed together, very loudly.

I breathed in the sweet smelling air that pervaded the holy temple of the secret seed. The light was dazzling. A hawk flew overhead as gulls cried passionately.

Here we are, earth again, dear brother!

Happy Solstice. Good Fortune Everyone (and me?)

December 26

A lonely day, even though Pilgrim will be around somewhere.

January 1

One central stem of the vipers bugloss stands upright, at least three feet towards the sky. Its metal green stem is covered with small, very dark brown spots. On the top of each spot grows a silky silver hair. Like two days growth on a grand-fatherly chin. From the stem grow flowers, each reaching upwards to the light. The flowers are totally remarkable: opening in succession up the central stem, each is a delicate bluey purple, with a deeper spot of stunningly bright mauve. Above the flowers already out, the stalk reaches forward like a snake's tongue, with each gland on its tongue producing a soft, seductive spike. When you brush your fingers over this upper stem, it parts and reveals the bright mauve spot of the as yet unopened flowers. It promises so much – and it delivers.

Around this central stem of flowers are splayed dozens of other stems, only these have fallen over, and then raised themselves up at some distance, creating a ring around the central stem of shorter ones, each similarly covered in these wonderful flowers. The whole effect is truly magnificent. I find myself floating above it and looking down at the mandala shape it creates. I have filled my circle with this and nothing but the truth.

I fall into her arms, merging. Around my central deep blue point will be spirals of blue and mauve energy, all supported by the green backdrop of our beautiful planet, for I will flower.

I'll tell you how it happened. Whilst sifting through some soil in a fairly untended area of the garden last summer, I found the small metal talisman. It slightly glinted in the early morning sunlight. Feeling very excited, I picked up the object for inspection. It was obviously man-made and appeared to be made of silver. I looked even closer at the small talisman, crafted carefully who knows when or by whom. I held in my hand for so long time passed but I remained.

The design was of a stylized hawk with an extension of his its held up in its beak. The hawk's left eye and a spot on its lower belly each contained a small red stone that turned out to be ruby.

I don't know why I did what I did, it just came to me. I put my hands linked together into the shape of a bird right over the talisman, then flapping my finger-wings I helped free it from all previous owners and attachments. Like releasing its soul, I made it mine.

The talisman looked beautiful. I kept staring at it, loosing myself in the thought-free fantasy it induced in me. With its image in my mind, in a flash I saw myself and everything in my vicinity as if held in the beak of a giant sized hawk. I felt myself sinking into a deep, warm reverie as the vision of being held in a hawk's beak brought me no fear. The hawk just is, I thought. I exist, the hawk exists. There need be no more. No more need. Then I realized something: looking closely at the talisman, the hawk's tail, which I had thought it held in its mouth, was decidedly a piece of viper's bugloss, not it's own tail at all. I was lost in it, unable to free myself from its hold. It became stronger then suddenly I was shouting out loud.

Wake up, I said to myself. Wake up! I repeated, louder.

I knew then the question to ask – not: who experiences all this? But from where does this experience arise?

I knew that at that precise moment, out in the garden, a female blackbird tugged a worm from the earth, wriggling in her beak. To hold and be held. The mystic marriage.

February 15

Through the gate I found the small blue and silver talisman. A bird face-shaped hieroglyph, sparking in the bright sunshine. Turned

Justice

around and looked behind, saw the carpet of violets vibrant in the bright sun. A few daisies are dotted amongst the violets, plus strands of dead, dried grass from year before. Snake-like with gouge smashed front, soul saved still inhabits the earth. Beautiful butterfly swoops then stops, closes its wings to me and the sun. Large eyes filled with water and multicoloured, spherical eyeballs brain, such immense proportions. We merge our bodies, our lives to the earth, become the earth in soul and body. And I brought the talisman back with me. Nothing before, just this.

I told Pilgrim all about it tonight, the whole mystery. Even she was surprised what I discovered. I want you to just watch how I told her. Some of what you see might be shocking, but it is something I really want to reveal to you. I told her it was going to deepen our relationship. And set something free in me. I told her it might be frightening, shocking even, and she was going to react to it, strongly maybe. It was frightening for me to show it to her.

I led her into a bedroom. We took off our clothes and lay together on the bed. My penis was bobbing, twitching into life. And I felt frightened because Pilgrim might find this too difficult to handle, but I didn't really think so.

Pilgrim told me she loved and trusted me, we had travelled in so many worlds together.

From under a pillow I pulled out the silver and blue talisman. On one side it bore a picture of the virgin Mary, on the other several letters in an unidentifiable script.

Look for your coin in the river where you lost it. That's where I found mine. Pilgrim and me, we embraced tightly, the talisman help between our hearts.

Tears welled up in her eyes. She told me it was here and I told her it is here.

A gate opened before us. The light shone so brightly from the other side we had to shield our eyes as we passed through.

Whether I've been here before or not is an attitude. Today I played an eager traveller, climbed a mountain and it bloody well serves me right that I'm exhausted! Phew! I had a sense of repeating something when I touched the bark of a tree that I have never touched before. How can two things be simultaneously true and untrue?

On my path were two broad strands of ivy, light one side, shadow on the other, each one climbing up a rather twisted beech tree. At the bottom I saw what looked like a figure, diving, wet with water, clasping to the bottom of the tree. Then above there was another figure, contortedly drawing itself up the first bank onto the shore of the tree, where there was a figure wearing an Assyrian headdress. This being, having made it out of the water, leaned against the tree, in the recovery position. Higher up the tree were a couple who were making love. She was stretching her arms up in the air, pushing her bottom out, and he was behind, entwined, with one arm around her waist, the other clasping the hairy inside of her armpit. Tightly pressed together, their bodies became a monkey climbing on the tree, looking very happy.

I wanted to reach the sunny clearing at the top of this hill where I knew I would be protected by the circle of ash trees. I'd be warm and able to bask in the setting sun. Ahead was a bird that looked like a penguin. It had a white front, a black back, stretched its head upwards, and waddled like a penguin does. As I got closer to it, it didn't move, it kept very still, and became a fallen tree, its side lying on the ground towards me. It bent upwards; one part of the tree, facing me, was light and stripped of bark, with green moss growing on it. The other side was in the shadow, moving away from me. When I came very close to the tree, I could see it was all the same colour. The illusion of shadow and light was just that – when I got close enough it was covered with moss and red fungus, one level of rot and decay building upon another.

Does the moss notices its existence, is it conscious? I am. Though eager to get to the clearing, I am taking in the sights.

The fallen leaves under the trees created a golden reddish glow, which illuminated the path as it twisted between trees and through an undergrowth made up of green plants with a spiral of five leaves at the top. I remembered again. I get caught up thinking about all the events in my life then I remember that this is my life, now. This is my life, now. And I'm thinking about what I'm doing with it. Sometimes we are not tuned in to our purpose and meaning, sometimes we get caught up and that is okay. Sometimes when I'm in it, it doesn't feel okay, but that's part of what life's about.

There is something edgy here today. Can I own this? I don't know what the world is waiting for. I'm waiting to move on, so I have to trust that, and move on. And enjoy this, whatever this is. I can enjoy being uncertain.

I will move on and stop being a resting place for weird insects.

I'm happy. No more secrets. In this is the revelation of all the teachings. There never were any secrets.

I stopped. There was the sound of footsteps walking on wet, stone steps, ascending out of a dark, wet passageway to the left of where I stood. The sound of dripping water synchronized with the footsteps. Hollow echoes filled the cavern.

There was the clanking of a large iron door.

A figure stepped out into the steamy gully. It was Pilgrim. I was pleased to see her, though shocked by her sudden but nonchalant appearance. Actually, Pilgrim was more amazed. She had assumed it was a little stream when she'd first encountered me. She could see now it was a wide, busy river we were looking down upon. We are gods and goddesses, aren't we?

With wet feet!

We were standing on the lovely hillside looking at a rainbow bridge across two sides of Manor Coombe. There were more hills behind, and a ruined town in the mid ground.

The rainbow, where it hit the gorge at that side, was very beautiful. We sat very still for a long while.

By the time we moved, the rainbow had disappeared and long shadows were being drawn over the hills by heavy rain clouds.

Like the wind, Pilgrim vaporized, leaving a sign of a horse's hoof and an arrow. Pointing to the pot at her end of the rainbow.

I followed a while, a long while, followed.

I stepped into the gateway.

Help me, shouted Pilgrim, somewhere just ahead.

The black maze, will we get to the centre?

What is your minotaur?

Pressing on, I pretended not to notice the question, all the time holding the hand of Pilgrim, pulling her along behind.

I found a small, cylindrical shaped bottle. I bent forward and picked it up.

Laughing, we stepped right through the gate, and burst into song.

When the pie was open,

Birds began to sing.

Now wasn't that a dainty dish

to set before a king.

That song has strong childhood associations for me.

I fished in a pocket and pulled out that small bottle. It looked like it just fell out of the sky.

We investigated it together. It's is a phial with a substance in it, with a label that says: mgn followed by what looks like numbers.

I opened the phial and looking inside could see it was filled with three or four drops of a thick purple liquid. I put it to my lips, then stopped and offered it to Pilgrim to sample first.

Haha, she refused so I put it to my lips and let one drop of the oily liquid drip onto my tongue. I saved the other two or three drops.

Everything changed then and there.

This world is one of adjustment, not justice, to bring us back to centre, synthesising love and will.

February 18

I was looking at the scarves in the shop in Cory. There were a couple of women in there who looked like a mother and daughter. The daughter was standing with her back to where I was with the scarves. To turn round the stand that the scarves were on, I had to actually touch the back of her hair. Lightly. She wasn't quite close enough to say excuse me, and also she was in conversation with her mother. So I never saw her, except her back. She was wearing a brown leather outfit: jacket and hat, all in brown leather. With light brown hair coming down around her head from under her hat, she looked a little weird. Her leather skirt was right down to her ankles, and she was wearing light brown leather boots under that, like a cowgirl.

Her mother, who was facing me, was talking to her all the time. They were in a conversation about whether these clothes were suitable for someone. They were saying a man's name – George – but what they were holding up were women's clothes. So that was kind of interesting. I got quite caught in this. Then I was aware I was actually touching her head and back whilst looking at these scarves. I'm thinking – why doesn't she turn round, or move or something.

Hanged Man

And the mother's face – she looked weird. They were both quite tall, the mother was as tall as me, certainly. She was in her sixties and her face was very lined, was quite bright, and she had a lot of makeup on. Not an excessive amount but quite a lot – more than average amount. She was very animated in the conversation.

The best thing of all. I noticed that there was an oval mirror on the wall behind the mother, and in the mirror I could see the face of the daughter who was standing in front of me. What was really astounding was she was watching me in the mirror. As I looked in the mirror I caught her. She'd been watching me, probably for a long time. Maybe all the time I'd been wondering why she wouldn't move or anything. So I see her face, and two things happen instantly. First of all I see she is very beautiful, a very pretty face, but god – she's made up in leather! Somehow her make-up it was kind of the same colour and look as her leather gear, you know, that yellowy sort of leather colour.

Her make up was the same colour as the leather she was wearing! With an amazing amount of black around her eyes. So these two black eyes in a brown face in this brown clothed body were staring at me in the mirror. It was like – wow! Well as soon as she saw that I'd seen her in the mirror, which was just like a second or so, it was very quick, she turned round and smiled. She was really nice.

I realised they were trans.

Remember those skirts, boy brother girl.

They both sound pretty weird, you know, the older woman with the lined face, the leathery face on the other one, with a lot of make up – and they were holding up women's clothes and excitedly talking about their suitability for George.

There was something right about that, something exaggerated about their looks. The other thing, though, is when I think of the younger one, the 'daughter', she was very attractive. In a second hand clothes shop, where better to find a trans person? You know now, it was me not you! You fool!

Phew – I then had a pile of women's scarves in my hands. I go over to the counter where there were – it was ridiculous – you won't believe this, either – there were four old ladies behind the counter. And they all involved themselves in serving me. Here I am, this man buying these women's scarves and they were all giggly. I don't know if they thought I was trans as well, but there was that atmosphere in the shop.

Fancy finding a mirror to watch me with. That is the mark of a certain quality in a person, all to do with images. The image of being a different sex, the image of clothes, and the image in the mirror. Hanging out, being upside down, inside out.

Yes, it is obsessed. There is something obsessive about that kind of camp, putting-on behaviour. It's like being in the grip of something, being driven by something, rather than just exploring it. I could want to feel sorry for people like that. And of course I'm often in the grip of something, driven too.

It's an interesting energetic experience, to do something like that. I can remember as a teenager my brother and I trying on some of our mother's clothes. We looked at each other in a mirror in various things, it was actually quite exciting, sexually exciting, erotic. I found it very erotic to look in the mirror and hitch my skirt up. In the mirror I was imagining my brother was a woman standing there, hitching her skirt up. So what I got off on was not the image of him wearing the skirt but the pretence I had a woman there. In my fantasy that was what I wanted. I don't think that is the same obsession as wearing women's clothes to become a woman yourself. That's a more internalised version of it. If you've taken that on, let it go, it was mine all along, not yours.

Sometimes it is difficult being a time traveller. Every thing is upside down.

February 28

If you say you are not interested in preaching to the converted it implies you are interested in preaching to the non-converted. Then the question is: who are these non-converted? Non-converted to what? Non-converted to your ideas about how the world should be? Non-converted to your belief in yourself as the supreme being?

Hi there, supreme being, you keep me hanging on – what have you got to say for yourself today?

The main thing I've got to say for myself is I am a re-al-ly very sexy person. After all, when you consider it, you are talking to the being who created the world. You can't get much sexier than that. The creator!

I'm a goddess floating in a sea of golden yellow and bright pink clouds. My most striking feature is my black eyes which are very dark, they can draw you into me.

I felt sexually and physically exalted as I looked into her eyes. It's like she's saying to me: I love you, take me, have me, join me, thrill me. Oh! We are One.

The image changed and I was back in the front living room of my childhood home.

Well they created us.

But then what am I for? Am I for sitting here looking at

this beautiful view, seeing seagulls flying over wet fields? Heavy rains, flooded fields, one particularly ploughed one is attracting large numbers of seagulls.

There was a sea of golden yellow and bright pink cloud above and near the horizon. Paranormal forces us to confront our fragility in the face of the unknown.

I fixed the image of the window. I looked out of it. My intent took me to the weir. I stood there looking around. I felt the cool air. I was still lying on the bed.

Strange female voices wailed in the background. Arabic.

I practiced projecting myself in this way, moving my energy body in and out the window. I learned it many years ago, but I still practice.

Other worlds get closer.

I am the editor. My job is to ensure the right information gets through. Therefore I also make sure the wrong information doesn't get through. I decide what is right and what is wrong.

I sound like a petty tyrant.

There's nothing petty about me, matey! I've got a very important job, I told you. I'm the creator. Listen. Cre-a-tor.

I protect you. I protect you from harm. I keep you safe. And then I tell you what's good for you.

Let me know it or see it, or feel it in some way if you are holding it back.

This is it, time to go now, fate awaits.

I was taken a long way down, into deep caves that felt damp yet strangely comfortable. A gentle but firm voice spoke into my ears.

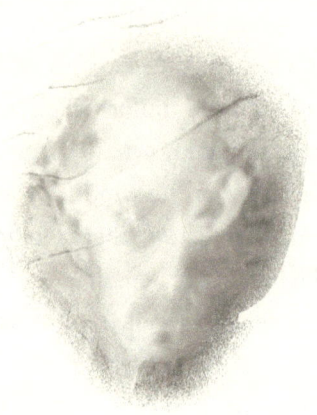

Death

No death too far away, some death here to stay. I am death. One day I will tap your left shoulder.

I felt a throbbing in my left shoulder. I'd advise you to succour and enjoy in the depth and breadth and height, every moment of your life. For I will come. It won't be a day too soon nor a day too late.

You all die at your time
    Use your breath. Breathe deeply.
    Drink water. Drink deeply.
    Make fires. Burn deeply.
    Come to earth. Love deeply.
    Create a soul, birth deeply each new day.
    For as the lord of death I also command the realm of birth. The image of me as a skeleton with a scythe is not an image

of me at all. Truly I am a beautiful naked woman lying in a sea of gentle waves that are part of and the whole of the ocean.

If you come to me as a child I take you in my arms and succour you at my breast.

If you come to me as a adult I take you in my arms and succour you against my chest, against my heart of fire that is not hell.

If you come to me as a priest I hold you tightly to my chest.

If you come as a lover I hold you tightly to my breast, oh child.

I drink your energy whatever way you come to me. Then I will take your energy like a sperm to fuse with one of my eggs to create the new being that you become.

This is the true image of death.

Your father feared your mother. Your mother feared your father. But they knew they were together to create you.

There was another long pause. Whose death energy merged with one of your eggs to create the birth that was me?

You come from a realm of guardian angels.

You are here to guard sacred places in your body and the land, and to be a seed of life.

I thought for a while then realised. To create. To create new worlds. I am the creator. To connect sperm with egg, sperm of power with egg of awareness.

I do believe death smiled.

Walk the land.

June 17

Three months since writing here because of what happened. Now I'm out in the world again. Thy will be done.

Climb down. Climb down, she said to me from the middle of unrest.

My mind just wandered.

I coughed strangely. I've got something very important to tell you. I'm going to tell it to you now and I'm never going to tell it to you again. So it's very important you remember it. So you do remember I'm going to just touch you by here. He bent across the table and just lightly touched me with his hand round the back of my neck. An overall feeling of calm came over me.

I trusted him completely, I had no reason not to. I liked his hand round my neck, where he touched me, Then he said, That's it. And you must always remember that. Now when I take my hand away you'll forget everything except that I've told you it.

I was confused. Then he took his hand away and I wasn't confused. I just knew something, something someone had told me before and I had forgotten before.

June 18

I noticed I'd got my right hand on the back of my neck. I pressed and as the tears came from my eyes, I remembered what he had told me.

I was really just remembering something, something I can't remember when I try but I know I remember it.

I wasn't crying but tears were pouring down my face.

We sat by the drive into what was probably a large house. A green hedge grew on either side of the drive, and another one next to the lane. The sun beat down on us. As well as having these strange tears pouring down my face, I felt shaky.

At that moment I reached over to touch Pilgrim on the back of her neck. To respond to her and to share the feeling with her. And so I could tell her.

Listen: I reached over and touched her, then moved my hand away.

I could tell by her expression that she had instantly forgotten what I'd just told her. It worked!

Only those who have been touched can.

Gosh, do I feel strange. It felt for a moment like someone was watching us. Witnessing us more like. I paused and looked round. Had we just forgotten something?

I was breathing quite heavily and I thought: what does it mean? Who was just touching my neck?

He said he was an alchemist but female, despite what his masks sometimes say. My star is like a cross in the heaven, he said. My constellation in the heavens is a cross, four visible stars creating the sign like an X at the height of your heavens. At the centre is a fifth star invisible to your sight and it is here I dwell. I am the ruler. They are many who are of us.

When you allow yourself to simply be yourself without trying to do something, but just letting it happen, then you are obeying my law. My law is the law of doing what you wish with the greatest of ease, for doing what you wish is what flows from you when you stop trying. Stop trying and obey my law. When your body dies, you can't maintain your body but you can continue. While you are alive you come in and out of different spaces, different dimensions as appropriate to your consciousness at that time. When you are with me in life you are in a space more than life for it includes death. In this space we can speak.

When you let the flow then you will know. If you try to be in my space then I am somewhere else. I am nowhere else when you are in my space. All I say is true without time. To be without time you let go into the intensity of any moment. Wipe the sweet sweat from the tips of your body. This is an elixir, to be with me.

It's like feeling every cell in your body sink relaxedly so it is no longer an effort to hold yourself up. So you can let yourself lie on the earth, letting go into my body, letting me support you, and then when you move you keep that same consciousness. Move now.

I held my bottle to the sky, then drank long and deep of the elixir, draining every last drop. I sang: There are four and twenty ways to look upon each day, and whatever anyone says, I will do it my way.

Then I saw the sign.

Thy will be done.

Climb down. Climb down, she said to me from the middle of unrest.

June 20

A green man with a necklace of red pearls smiled as he opened the gate. Peace be to all who enter herein. We have prepared the pathways and cleared the gullies. We have shaped the peaks and rounded the hills, for this is the time of the new moon. Each of the red jewels on my necklace is a sun. Around each of these suns rotate many planets.

Let me warn you to be aware of my sister who also wears a necklace of red suns. Look more closely when you meet her and see her suns are in fact skulls covered with the bright menstrual blood of her death body. Smile when she speaks to you, and speak softly, for then you will be like me, a guardian.

Thanking the green man, I stepped through the gateway.

The air was filled with the whining of machinery, somewhere – everywhere in the distance. It wasn't deafening, but it continually intruded on my consciousness. It sounded like thousands of people using electric saws.

This is not what I was expecting, I thought. This world was a mixture of yellows, lime greens, oranges and browns.

The bodies of dead snakes lay strewn either side of the path. The sound in the distance was now more high pitched, interspersed with knocking, hammering sounds. The bodies of snakes that had slithered up smooth, tall tree trunks, wrapping their bodies together around one another as they climbed upwards towards the pink and grey sky, lay still.

The sound of machinery in the distance shows that there are other beings in this world, but where I am, there are few other creatures. At the moment.

As I climbed higher, the sound of the machinery became more distant but was still insistent to my ears. At this higher altitude, there was the distinct sound of howling wind. I lit a fire inside my belly. This is the place where alchemy begins and ends. The place where strange creatures wrap themselves like folded pancakes, charred and folded in the recesses of the mind.

At that moment, at the edge of the sound, I heard the heartbeat of some other creature.

It's cold here, a voice said.

I looked round, wondering who had spoken. There was the sound like that of a woodpecker in a tree, just above the level of my head. The wind howled louder.

It's cold here, it repeated.

I kissed the air.

Welcome to our world, said many creatures all around.

Welcome to my world, I replied. Three times round the meadow I ran, dipping my head on every third step as if I would crash into an invisible barrier if I did not. After finishing the third circle, I swung once and clutched the trunk of a smooth snake-covered tree, then stepped forward to embrace the grandmother and grandfather of this holy place.

I chanted as I walked in a spiral, backwards, from grandmother to grandfather. This place is the place of spells. Leaning against grandfather, I looked at the distant, sharpened peaks and rounded hills, peering through the tops of trees that shed leaves like a rainstorm of flashing lights.

This is such a place! A place to stop and be. The more I looked into my own mind the more I saw the black branches and branchlets of the trees silhouetted strongly against the pink and grey sky.

What am I here for?
To bring yourself out.
To place ourselves within.

I decided to walk on from grandfather. Slowly and carefully I trod over the moving ground. My breath was heavy to my ears, louder than the distant machines and howling wind. I looked down into a ravine, strangely recognised as a place I'd been before but now could not recall when or how or with whom.

How the world always changes, and always remains the same, I thought.

There was a wailing of voices, ever louder.

Is this my dream? Is this someone else's dream?

June 21

Summer solstice.

Find your bliss, follow the bliss you find in your dream, for your dream is the concrete reality of the many worlds. Unlike your apparent waking reality, which is but one dream in the many worlds.

I walked upwards, climbing slowly and breathing more heavily. I felt quite weak in my stomach. I continued walking wearily, and yet I also felt rested at the same time. What is this weariness, what is it that compels me to drop to my knees, to all fours, to roll onto my side, close my eyes and drift into dream? My words were lost as I did just that, dropping softly onto a pile of dead leaves.

There was no answer, and if there had been I wouldn't have heard it. At that moment, I slipped into an adjacent dream world.

The alchemy is happening.

Turning left, I found myself facing the most awe inspiring creature I had ever seen. With a small strong body well rooted into the earth, it was many different colours of green. The creature's head was rounded, with one eye on the left, peering straight at me, and two enormous multi-branched antlers, reaching into the sky. Come ahead, the creature said.

I stepped forward, closer to the eye of the creature. It stood still, feeling no fear, or any other reaction, to my presence. It was empty.

I stepped closer, and touched the right hand antler as I peered deeply into the single left eye of the creature. I am Pan, I am birth, he said. I open my crown and invite you to enter.

The wailing voices suddenly stopped. There was still the sound of distant machinery and winds, but they were slight.

Pan commanded me to dip my finger into the green matter. I did so, then shook a drop into the creature's eye and a drop on my head.

I felt a great strength in my body. Everywhere on my body all the hairs stood on end. Goose pimples pricked in waves of delight and fear across my naked body. The wind howled loudly. I am naked. In this dream I am Pan. Open Open. Open.

The wind stopped. There was complete silence.

June 22

Temperance

This is the dream of the internalised body. This is the dream of the holy alchemy.

Upwards and onwards, ever upwards, onwards. Upwards and onwards into and beyond earth.

Here. This is a place where angels meet those they watch, and beings meet their guardians.

I filled my lungs with the sweet air. I listened intently to the sweet chorus surrounding me.

This is the alchemy of earth angels, step from one to the other.

This is the age of earth alchemy, step from the other into the one. This is the earth of age alchemy. Step into yourself, and out of the dream.

I knew what to do. Facing the east, I inhaled the air, held my breath for a count of thirty three, and blew the trance-formed and muted breath of Pan to the east. With praise tapped three times.

I turned to face the south, inhaled, held my breathe for a count of sixty-six and breathed out the fire of the holy god Pan.

My eyes blaze with the creation of new worlds.

I turned to face the west. I inhaled, held my breathe for a count of ninety-nine, and exhaled. The waters of life flow from the reified pores of my holographic body.

I peered into the water and felt no fear.

I turned to face the north. I inhaled, and held for a count of one hundred and forty two. Holding my breathe was an effortless joy. I exhaled soul through my soles into the earth. My girth became the diameter of the earth. I was filled with molten metals, and the joyous cries of those who were filled with awe at the sight of the inner earth.

Conjoined with the outer soul. This is alchemy.

I turned back to the east, circled to the south, the west, and then to the north. From whence I came there is no return. I move forward into the life of a living soul.

Bending my knees, I bowed slightly and acknowledged the existence of Other.

Finally I turned back to the east. And I spread the ashes west, south, west, north, east.

Now I walk into the unknown depths of this newly healed world of light. This is my soul. All this I see, hear, sense, feel, is my soul. It is virtuous reality.

Later:

My magical memory was operational for a while after coming back so I quickly wrote these down, a series of meditations based on my experiences of being a time traveller, trying to reify them in this world:
– Bless everything.
– This is my life, now.
– Have I forgotten something?
There is a very interesting and precise way of looking at connecting with your heart, your soul, your centre. It has been described as conscious work to create a soul. You are not born with a soul, or if you are you still have to activate it in some way.

The world goes on irrespective of me (and you.)

June 25

To remind me to remain on earth, a small green stork-like creature nipped me just above my right knee, then ran off, cackling. The elixir from the wound ran through my body as I trod over fields of horse mushrooms. They were so tightly bunched, I had to step on their tops. They took my weight as I stepped forward, stumbling, then righting myself. The healing was complete – the wound had opened.

There is the sound of a great flapping of wings. Long brown insects scurried away at the instance the sound left my belly.

Feathers dropped all around me as a multitude of birds flapped out of the trees.

I am only human. The irony of my statement is immediately apparent to me. I am only human. I can see them all now, surrounding me, playing joyously. A freedom came to my step. A strength to my body. Silken curtains parted before me, each world I passed through like a rapid momentary flash of beauty followed by another then another.

I stepped into a wide open space, bathed with a light green and crimson red light.

Gosh, I think I've been here before. Yes, it's the earth.

It's the earth, The most beautiful garden. Oh mother earth, planet earth, embrace me.

Hello.

The earth was a magnificent brown colour. Wet from a recent downpour of refreshing rain, it was now ablaze with light, as the sun emerged from behind clouds and lit the day with glorious colours.

This is truly the place to be.

June 30

Light the fires for Pan.
Cross the water for Pan.
Breathe the air for Pan.
Ride the back of a serpent down through the aethyrs,

come to earth and be with the eaters. Become an earth creature, for Pan.

I danced with the creatures. And with pan pan pan, my pan, I open.

Once more I ran three times round the meadow before collapsing, panting for breath on a mound of soft earth. I die. I undertake an operation of the magician's art. I invoke Pan. I am Pan. I open.

I make the transition between death and the devil. I accomplished the magician's art. I open, I open, die die die, I can go down –

In my freedom I choose with sorrow and sadness and reluctance but also with open armed freedom – I choose to step through the gate into the dark tunnel.

I stepped through the gate and came face to face with the dark goddess. This dark goddess is so beautiful. I am looking in her eyes and to look into her eyes is to melt into bliss. I am Pan, as I slide into her openness. I come inside you. A bird sings. You are lying on your belly beneath me. I part your cheeks gently, I hold the top of your thighs as I come inside you. My body is arched like a bow. The arrow is pulled back, fully tensed.

You are my secret heart. The whole of my shot I dedicate to you, my body quivering with the tension of the arrow at the bow at your backside. You make circular movements with your hips and look back over your shoulder.

She came, smiling softly, staring into my eyes. My body ached as her wet, juicy tongue slithered out between her upper teeth and red lower lip. Her pink, slippery tongue looked as if she was about to lick the surface of a wet strawberry then sink her teeth into its flesh. I adore you. All of us adore you. Look into my eyes. Heal me all around you.

My eyes watered as I slowed my movements and sank into the pulsing togetherness of our two bodies.

Let go into me. This is alchemy. My breast hold, breathe told secret art lips. Drink of me and you with splendid abandon.

I come into her, sweetly.

Show me your true face.

I am me and you are me. You are you and I am you. What we see in each other is a reflection. If we both choose to see our beauty, oh yes.

I could see a very beautiful young woman with strong masculine features, dark eyes and shining teeth. Her very, very dark black eyes peered right into me, telling me to move closer.

Still riding the back of a serpent down through the aethyrs, dance with the creatures, for Pan.

With open open, my Pan, I open, I sang. This goddess is so beautiful, I am looking in her eyes and to look into her eyes is to melt into bliss. I am Pan, as I slide into her openness. A bird sings. You are my secret heart.

She came, smiling softly, staring into my eyes. I adore you. All of us adore you. Look into my eyes. Heal me all around you. This is alchemy. My breast hold, breath told secret art lips. Drink of you and me with splendid abandon. Show me your true face.

We merge in alchemical purity,
And part in equal purity of art.

Still riding the back of a serpent down through the aethyrs, will this be repeating for ever, will I ever get through? Do I even want to?

July 23

One year of keeping this my final diary.
Yes, I know now when I will die.
Through the gates of matter, there is usually only silence.

I marvel at the opulent splendour of the world I am in.

The devil spoke. Sometimes when I'm feeling devilish, I look down on the world below through one of the holes in my floor. Right now I'm looking through a particular hole where there are silver ladders and scaffolding, and brightly coloured clothes and very long sticks resting against the scaffolding. Right down on the ground there is a multitude of people, very small seeming from up here. There's a bunch of them who, although they don't know it, from up here I see them making the shape of a five petalled flower at the centre of which is an illuminated being. The energy of the illuminated being is creating this pattern amongst the people around without their being conscious of it. When I look down from up here, and am feeling devilish, I think: Gosh. There's a somebody like me. And I bless that person.

Where he lived was a paradise of abundance. All the walls are covered with multicoloured clothes with beautiful patterns, symbols, mandalas, Egyptian, Indian, western cloths, beautiful rich velvet carpets in shades of deep red which pleased my eyes.

And they call it hell. The devil laughed until he fell backwards, clutching his sides, and rolled luxuriantly on one of his rich carpets. His laughter became thunder in the heavens.

Devil

Clambering over to another hole in the floor, he looked through. He bellowed. His spit was like a torrent of rain below.

I could see a very beautiful woman, auburn hair cascading over her shoulders. She had soft but piercing eyes, lips made red with swathes of lipstick. There was a slight edge of wateriness in her eyes. She seemed to draw me into her dream.

The devil is dreaming of the pregnant Mary, mother of Jesus.

Looking down on her, I could see there was a gap between the bottom of her light coloured top and her green skirt, revealing her rounded belly, full of child. Warm legs, warm thoughts, smooth flesh.

The Devil yearns for her, but he doesn't have her, he cannot have her. I have made love with her, though. The angel Gabriel appeared to her and she was bedazzled.

We all asked the same questions. Who is the virgin? Who is this? Who is Gabriel? Who is the devil? Who am I?

We all came to the same answer.

July 28

The feathers of a dead bird were lying on the path in front of Pilgrim and I. The bird's flesh had been eaten away and the feathers had gently dropped into the shape of the bird.

We were ambling through a rich meadow. There were some mature teasels, very tall in the middle of the meadow. It was such a wonderful meadow birds singing, very beautiful, insects, sunshine. I've never really related to this place before.

Brilliant. Wonderful. Abundant. Wonderful!

But the pollen was really affecting my mouth, and I needed to leave. I am going through this gate.

An ancient looking, wizened being stood directly before me, his eyes like large pools of murky water. Oh lord, I want to go to heaven, heaven is all I want to be. There are churches of commerce, we build the highest sculptures to the industrial god, this is a personal statement, ego, not connected to the planet, except physically, we are autonomous spirits.

I looked around me. I was entering an ancient forbidding town, falling down. It was beautiful, overgrown, with big stones, like a dream. The upper stories of all the buildings were crumbling. Like old castles, with naked men and women dancing in deliberately high towers of impregnability.

The ancient being spoke softly. Ideally floors have no windows, this is reassuring, nobody can get into there. All around stood male symbols, phallic fantasies, sequenced in citadels of feminine moons. We go into the place where the place of the earth is woman. I see you are loving Mary. The virgin is a tower of ivory, an enclosed and walled garden, the magic woman.

I have made love with Mary and found her name is also infinite space and infinite stars.

Tower

The tower of ivory, sealed, was opened from her fast impregnability by mine own angel spirit. Fertile earth mysteriously creating truths. My grimoire of liberal truth is a tower of sexual strength, female and male equal.

I felt strangely empowered by the voice of the ancient being and found myself merging into the energies of this place. A father makes a tower of strength out of a daughter's virginity, so to preserve her chastity and his erection.

We are all children of priceless princesses, of many Marys. Mother invite me in, daughter invite me in.

She always chooses when.

July 29

The virgin soul is precious, nothing good enough, the whore soul the same but nothing bad enough, and they are the same, what is, is, Isis is. My self is sun sullied by real life transactions passing just in front of the gate where I await entry. The tower looks different from anything else, and of a different age but it blends in so quietly and obscurely most people pass without seeing it. Aliens see it, but they don't believe in towers.

Looking deep into the being's large eyes, I saw the murkiness fade to reveal clear pools of pink light. Open the gate and let me into the tower. Most people never enter. I wonder what it is like inside.

The gate was opened and in the very same moment I found myself both standing where I had been looking up at the tower and standing atop the tower looking down. I like looking down on you, I like you looking down on me, I like looking different ways. Security is a fisheye lens in the door. The red cross painted against the angel of the lord.

Like shifting attention from the head to somewhere else in the body and then you see yourself as you are, protected by the tower.

The tower offers security, through connection rather than disconnection, though. Its castle-like shape warming even a heart of stone. It is total. Insulating. A bisexual environment abstracted into the last years of a person's life, for a tower is a song in the heart that is closed to the ears of youth.

I heard the sound of footsteps coming up the tower steps.

The ancient being's voice rose from below, with a tone of warning. Dark horses in dark towers. There is the place for meditation, deep in the earth for one hundred days every year.

This is the place where the devil tempts Christ, recharging his batteries with the refusal. I realised I had had to come up into the tower to do that.

On Jesus's tomb the inscription said: grant me to be remembered for who I am, not what they say of me.

I fell to my knees and prayed. The fountainhead, the maidenhead, pure virgin tower.

The demon never came, she came to me instead, and we had sex in the tower.

There was a crescendo of orchestra music as we came together. I have touched heaven.

There was a long silence, inner and outer, broken only by my occasional thoughts.

I am not downtrodden, I am in the earth, dreaming of climbing towers, and climbing towers of dreams.

I remembered the recurring dream from my childhood, with the tower I was climbing over and over, always to finally squeeze through a narrow passage into the light.

A clear voice inside me spoke of miracles. Detach in the tower and remember there is so much to do. Abstract and pull away, like a mind overdone with towering intellectualism.

Don't do it, be it. Allow all possibilities.

Go up the tower in a lift, let yourself see below, then remember to come back down, only not the same way. Confused? You bet I was.

Have you ever felt comfortable in a tower? I don't have victims. Look down there. Would you pity one of those people you see as minute dots far below if it stopped moving?

I knew the demon was tempting me. God is in man, not out there, or up there. The old spirit and soul of fire is being burnt up, water wishy madness, blocks of towers, towers of blocks, begone in the howling wind. Come my Mary.

She appeared, brightly. She raised her arms in the sign of the crescent moon (a magical pass she had possibly taught Pilgrim) and the demon disappeared.

Now Pilgrim was standing before me. It was her or me, and I stepped forward into her arms. (Well, I will soon).

August 1

This is a beautiful place, a good place to let go of the past and move into the future, as we ran faster and faster.

Near the bottom of the slope we came to a holy brook. The sound of the water alone was enough to cleanse the heart.

What an amazingly blessed feeling comes into my heart as I walk towards this brook. I am blessed. We are blessed. You are blessed.

Sun blessed!.

Right. Quiet. Just be here now. Stop rehearsing, be here. Stop being the wardrobe mistress. Be here. Stop being you or anyone or anything. Be here. You don't have to whisper or shout.

You don't even have to talk.

You can stop thinking.

Stop now.

We walked on silently, magically into fairyland.

August 23

We had both been excitedly anticipating the meeting, because of events that had happened in our lives.

I was walking along, you know, like I do, and I came across a very warm, relaxing, meadow filled with beautiful scents, quite mesmerizing. I just sat down and basked in the warmth and beauty of the place. Took my clothes off, laid in the sunlight, warmed my body, and half dozed.

I had a dream where a woman very similar to Pilgrim only different and blond came to stand naked besides me. This startled me when I woke up – this was all in the dream – so I stood up very fast, then felt giddy. We embraced, and as we embraced, I realized that she was the virgin Mary, or so I thought. I said to her, I asked her, and she replied that – these were her exact words – Mary and mary.
Well we had this beautiful experience, it was like but not making love and like but not exchanging energies. I think I can honestly say I made love with Mary and mary, the Mary who is all and everything who is also the mary here now.

Pilgrim joked that she thinks I might have got there before Gabriel, or I was Gabriel, that's what it seemed like. What a laugh.

Star

It isn't anything else, its just what it is, everything. It's the shekhinah, the shakti, the indwelling presence of the immanent goddess in us all.

Right now. Here. This is it.

Within us. Within us.

This is it.

The light is turning dark. I've put the light on already and the air itself is still black.

Oh my goddess!

September 22

The equinox comes round again and a happy Celtic crossing round the bushes to everyone and everything. Harvest. The word is ending now.

Sometimes I've been very negative about religion but what I'm aware of now is so-called religion is only a form of, something in the name of religion. There are other kinds of religion. Esoteric, meaningful religion that is a very interesting and precise way of looking at connecting with your heart, your soul, your centre. It is about becoming centred on your heart, then you grow your soul. Of course, it's then what emerges from your heart that makes the difference. Care for others arises.

I would like to call that something else.

I like being in the present time but in different places – it's space-time travelling really. We all travel in time because even in the present moment we are inevitably travelling on. The best time travel takes place in the present moment.

Always staying in the present moment –
    Being here immortally.

So today I am an immortal embodying as a time traveller disguised as a tourist disguised as a totally non-hasslable tourist.

The present movement, going with the flow. You can only flow if you allow yourself to come into the present moment. When you are off on fantasies about what you are going to do tomorrow, or what you are going to eat next week, then you're not flowing. Or if you are off in the past, worrying about what you feel guilty about, or what pleasured your senses, then you are not flowing. In the present moment you can feel sad about something to do with the past, or you could talk about future possibilities. You could be sad to contemplate something that's going to happen in the future, because we know tomorrow and next week, unless things change in a way, there will be animals and people that will be downtrodden, hungry and abused. So in the present we feel sad and angry.

You know in that sense the world goes on irrespective and irrelevant of us. It's important that as immortals we engage with the world, yeah. When you come to a place as a human being, you engage with it, you don't just flip off out again. You sometimes stop being a tourist and become something else - like me now, for instance, being a dentist in Bulgaria.

September 23

Moon

I remember that huge full moon the very first time Pilgrim and I walked down the hill above Le Chateau. We had it beating on us all night long. It was so powerful it drove us both crazy. It was so strong.

In my memory, I'm mystified by the double moon image, it appears as if a second one is moving next to the first one. This is a strange planet we live on. It's our strange planet, oh Pilgrim.

The most beautiful woman in the world is the goddess, always. Dear brother, now you know the truth, if you are with a woman you know who she is. Let it be. Let it rest in your hearts. You can join us later. That's very frightening and exciting, especially considering … you know!

In a way it is because we connect into her that we are okay here, we are successful in our walking. It's a real affirmation. We commune with the land and worship the goddess. Maybe I'm getting omnipotent now!

I like sitting at the table of the lord, Arthur's round table. I like the archetype behind that, the idea of a circle, and an elect, not in a nasty hierarchical sense, an elect rather than an elite. People who are elected by their spiritual nature on some level to be sitting at this table, in this circle, which is working with the energy of the always a virgin. I picture thirty six characters at the table. It's so abstract its hard to put words on it. There are certain people there I know, so it has definitely got form.

On the earth they might take other forms rather than people.

It's good to engage with the earth, it's sad if we loose our contact with the other worlds. Its about using your energy as a tool to buy you time to engage in the world. And we all die. . . so is there anything better than sitting here, looking at this beautiful moon?

A bat flew between Pilgrim and I and the moon.

You know, this beautiful light in this room now, it's silver and blue, it's like god.

Hello bat, come and eat all the insects. I saw the bat fly over the face of the moon.

Even the dung beetle is beautiful. There is a hand reaching to the moon now, with fingers.

Life's not that strange, not really.

November 14

I yearn for you, my earth, to fill my hands with your warm brown
blood. Open up to the free flowing blessing
of the totally uninhibited light: the blue sky is always here.
Living it.

November 18

You can only flow if you allow yourself to come into the present
moment.

Not today after all. Soon, my lord.

December 25

Happy Birthday me!

January 1

Happy year, is it? Sad year is it? Neither year is it? Whose there?

Pilgrim says to work magic you bring archetypes through to an
astral level. It's very powerful magic that she doesn't usually talk
about. Part of me is reticent to tell you.
        I feel a bit frightened in my solar plexus. Anxious.

Real magic is choosing and focussing on where you arise from then making it imaginal. Rather than fantasy images, constantly changing, like Eve in the garden, or Julius Caesar or Abraham Lincoln, you let the form change but you stay true to the originating energy. It changes its form, but it is always the same. For me, just now, it is: the most beautiful woman in the world, the whole world.

Of course Pilgrim is her. And every woman. Even you and I, inside, brother, are absolutely one hundred per cent her on this manifest level. On the astral level she's every woman and all women – and no women because she's constantly changing form. The most beautiful woman in the world is just a term that describes this infinitely wide, energetic sea of bliss energy. Energy of pre-manifestation. Then like going back to the animal, an instinctual level, it's what we come out of, the earth.

The mother, the vagina, the egg, the spark, the arising. The place of original magic.

Take for instance, Maria, our little sister, the goddess of the leaves: she is alluring, she is seductive, she controls time, she slows time, she stops time, for the inhalation of the inspiration of love; the intoxication of joy and rapture; the exhilaration of the senses; the exhalation of the energy of love. She opens the space between moments; she has the sweetest of scents, our little sister, the goddess of the leaves.

We were sitting on the earth by a stone. I had my hand on the earth. There wasn't really anything there but it felt like there was an opening, it felt like it was an opening that if I looked I'd see a little crack in the earth, an opening going into a hole. Of course when you looked there wasn't any crack there or anything like that. I realised something I already knew, but it become clearer through this experience. Mother earth. Gaia. The vagina from whence we all came and to which we all return.

There has been some kind of change in the earth energy recently. It's a good change. It's about dreaming. The earth is, at this moment, accepting our dreams. She is absorbing our dreams. For quite a long time she has been rejecting our dreams.

All you do, it is just walking the land, and dreaming.

It's more on the conscious-unconscious level, the contact place between the two, between physical and astral. Where you are going into or coming out of dreams.

It is on that edge, out walking the land. Taking magical walks.

It's about a shift in consciousness, planetary wise.

Pilgrim, the reason you are the most beautiful woman in all the worlds in my life is because I have manifested you. In my dream that is one hundred per cent true.

As well as your wound, your wounding is also part of why you are a woman. It's a gift coming from your heart.

Being wounded, opened in a particular way, energises your dream. It doesn't reify it, but it energises it. To reify means bringing it into manifestation, making it into a thing. Your wounded heart, the energy of that is about the wounding energising your dream rather than reifying it. It's not coming into manifestation, so your wounding energises your heart. That's not the whole story, just part of it. This is astral manifestation rather than manifestation on the physical. On the physical level you are not reifying your dream, so that energy has to go somewhere, so it goes into the astral and into your heart. It pushes energy up, straight up the spine to the heart, so that energises your heart to – to get you to be a person actively engaged in the process of creating a soul. The heart connects with the soul. It matches.

January 4

I enter the dark inner seascape of copulating male bodies. Out of the depths of this place my brother emerges.

He would pause for a few moments at most, during which I would strain in every pore of my body to come.

Help me come, Jesus!

Well I think maybe once or twice I came, but of the dozens and dozens of times we must have done it, I usually gave up, with softening parts, unable to bear the onslaught of my own impatience and fear and disgust with myself.

January 6

When I was still in my teens I wrote this for you:
You are through, we will show you breath like flames from witches mouths,
thin wispy children flying dragon kites, voices calling from sunset pictures,
a wilderness of meteors shredding and pale, clouds of summer

crickets, cottages covered in twilight colours,
empty river beds and chilly winter eves, leaves in showers of dancing pigeons,
marble fields through crystal windowpanes, laughter in clear skies and corridors of milk frost – everything you desire.

January 18

Sun

The passing of moments so slow, we stop to look within you and are caught by your beauty, then we pass and each moment stands alone in the past. Just like the clouds pass the sun, sometimes they are done and gone. Life is real then, only when I am. Stop the wheel!

Exquisite perfection, and utterly alien: a flower.
Bleeding stars, kala stars, heart blood, merging. It is through the flesh. Energy through a straight line, sunbeam. And children sing

of sunshine, endless beams of blue cosmos where we are one, we are none. You better believe: the blue sky is always here, the warm earth is always here.

Alive today.

I will awaken to my heart forever; I will to awaken. And I close my eyes to see you there in all your forms, my glorious goddess. Awaken my earth, my body, awaken and sing.

January 21

The back lanes on the way home! Do you remember them? It is like now, whatever you experience now is the same as the back lanes back home. Have you got it yet?

There were some kids – a gang of which I was a member – who had been exploring the back lanes behind the houses in the streets of the city where we lived. There was a mysterious maze of these narrow worm-like lines of energy that moved their way behind the houses and between the roads, always there yet often mysteriously changing direction, or splitting into several different paths going in different directions, or in one case even encircling a triangular area attainable only by the lanes.

This triangular area was my greatest find. It had some very old buildings in it, a mysterious looking garage door with ancient wood, and what at one end looked like an old small factory, derelict, with cracked wood walls, flaking bits of paint and perhaps a bit of a name plate. The mystery was when you stepped inside.

I let others show me the lanes that they knew and I excitedly discovered many new places, but I knew they wouldn't get to the triangle.

When I first took my brother there, he hugged me and I hugged him and we were both delighted. My delight was greater, knowing he would also soon find out about the mystery inside, and he was already praising me for the greatest find.

Oh glory to God in the high. As you stepped, stepped into the ground floor room of the factory, you entered what was in fact the ground floor room of the inner palace, the cathedral of lights. And glory be to the goddess. I'd learned of her first in this very place.

Our bodies of light came together with a sizzle as we leaned together to breath the brotherhood of man. From the inside, the windows of the building, rather than being cracked and dirty, were four large cathedral windows. They were made of stained glass in rainbow effects of all the brightest colours, every colour imaginable. All in little squares up the window, with patterns, and sweeping effects of colour.

All four windows shone so brightly it was as if there were four suns in the sky, each beating through a window with an intense light. When you looked higher up, through the broken edges of wood where the upper floor had crumbled away and broken, you could see the vaulted arch of the beautiful painted ceiling, eight miles high.

We looked in one anothers' eyes intently and we learned how to direct the left, right, middle and double gazes. Later, that same day, we learned another secret. We learned to hold one another tightly, letting the throbbing pulse of blood between us dictate the rhythm of squeezing. We combined this with our eye gazing and connected breathing. We travelled through dimensions of space and time.

We also learned how to catch our breath just at the moment of the pulse and to synchronise this gap in our breathing, whilst maintaining our gaze. All this was heaven. And we entered that holy place as frequently as we could.

February 1

Candlemass, the day for making love to Bridget the goddess of yearning for the summer. Open to me, sez me! (Pilgrim)

Maybe at times we loved one another. We had the experience of the triangle. Wherever you are whatever you are doing, I wish you well, and breathe away now any bad connections. That was the last technique we learned in the secret cathedral of the triangle, to breathe away bad connections with people, breathing them out into the four directions, picturing the stained glass windows absorbing the negative energies and turning them to light.

Why did I hold onto them for so long? I breathe the four fold breath, then I breathe in the released energy, easily and freely.

I say adieu to my old life.

Judgement

February 4

These are feelings of hope and the expression of pleasure. What god do they connect with?

There are two male children playing, halfway up a green hillside. At the top of the hill is the womb, and the womb is walled away from these male children. They dance on their side of the wall, awaiting their chance for that wall to dissolve and for them to form relationships with woman, the goddess.

Active to passive. Passive to active.

February 19

I stopped. There was the sound of footsteps walking on wet, stone steps, ascending out of a dark, wet passageway to the left of where I stood. The sound of dripping water synchronised with the footsteps. Hollow echoes filled the cavern.

There was the clanking of a large iron door.

And then I thought, here it is again, the repeating pattern. I've been here before, I've heard that iron clank before. What is this? Whatever, I knew that Pilgrim would now appear and sure enough she did.

Just ahead of us were some rapids. Stepping over the rapids, onto the other side, we could hear the sound of rushing water now as we became smaller and found ourselves walking along a path at the river's edge.

Somebody had dropped the blue and silver talisman with its embedded rubies. Pilgrim bent over and picked it up.

I'm giving birth, she said excitedly. Well, not exactly. Her tone was somehow both sad and joyous at the same time. She had found the gate that takes her back to where she started. It was our farewell.

It took a moment for it to sink in.

Back to where she started. I wanted to go with her, for her to show me, but I knew. I knew.

February 25

I stepped through a gate alone and found myself in a small back yard behind a row of terraced houses. On a low wall at one end a woman was lying in the sun.

I said hello, but she was far away in her thoughts and didn't notice I was there.

Even in the 50s, her blonde hair seemed rather strange, contrasting so starkly with her black eyelashes and black eyebrows.

Her body was lumpy and interesting. I wasn't the only man there looking at her. I've got a hard on, said my brother.

She woke to that, said she noticed it, pulling her earrings off and closing her eyes into thin slips as she stared hypnotically into his eyes. Her pouty lips and her teeth were all giving him the same message.

I'd seen it all before in those b-rated fifties films – that's all you did see before it faded into another grim scene of distasteful mistrust, lies, prejudice and moral lassitude. Burdened already by signs of urban decay, none of them seemed to be noticing, somehow.

My father noticed what everyone else noticed at the time. The bulge in his pants flicked away as we watched the movie. I knew what he would fantasize about that night.

March 6

The music was dramatic. The voice spoke loudly, his tinny voice bellowing from the cheap speaker. He told me he thought I thought he was stoned when he said he'd seen the old man. His voice rose with greater passion. My brother: he told me he had seen dad who was asking for me a few minutes ago. He spoke in a calm voice, sounding like he was trying to convince himself more than me. Then I was coming down the stairs and I saw dad at the bottom, like an evil apparition, beckoning me to join him in hell. I tell you, it's true. There was a strange buzzing sound filling up everywhere. Inside and outside my head.

The old man's face is getting on my nerves. Dad's face would get on anyone's nerves, with his rolling left eye.

I tried to reason with him but it was no good.

He looked perplexed, angry, confused – the emotions playing across his face, contorting it, making his left eye roll like only dad could do. What have you done with the moment?

It was the only thing to do. I had to get rid of it. Every moment is in synch with every other moment, so I forgot the lot.

But what about the moments in between?

What do you think we've been living in?

My brother said they were his moments too. I killed for them, he insisted. He was raging, out of control. He lunged at me with a knife.

Just then dad came back into the room. Is this a private fight or may your father which art in heaven join in?

We stopped fighting instantly. The room was chilled and there was the humming sound that surrounded him, filling the room.

Dad said he had a surprise for us. We've arranged a little celebration, he said in an evil voice.

You are going to be the guests of honour.

My brother shouted to get out and moved closer to the apparition.

Dad just disappeared.

He can't do anything. He's dead.

March 17

I couldn't help noticing that she had a very sexy body. As I said, lumpy, true, but it looked like it would envelop you, hold you warm, tight. She had an archetypal juiciness about her.

She asked us to take her away from there. I wouldn't be any trouble to you. We'd get along all right. This would all be something to remember afterwards.

She said our father in heaven means nothing to her now.

Well he does to me. Doesn't anybody mean anything to you? You only care until a better proposition comes along.

She said: You can say what you like to me, but you can't change me and you can't hurt me either. I am the goddess, even in this form. I've no pride where you are concerned and I don't give up easily. I never had a home. I never had a father. I never had a thing, until you came and found me in the holy cathedral.

That day I found I was attractive to the opposite sex, I discovered my legs weren't made just to stand on. I had one talent, most people haven't got any. So I used that talent and I got tough. I never loved anyone until you came along. I was never unfaithful to anyone in my life because I never had anyone to be unfaithful to. Please take me.

Universe

Oh, what's the use? We are not nice people, let's stop playing cat and mouse. I put my arms around her and we embaced passionately.

At that moment, our father in heaven came back in. I went to excuse myself.

He was fuming.

Both of you go to hell he said to us. I felt like saying the same to him.

Never mind, let him go, she said, clinging to me.

I kind of realised then it wasn't just a sexy woman in my arms, it was my mother, our mother, all mothers. She looked at me calmly, calculatedly.

I ran after him, out to where he was angrily getting the car out of the garage.

I begged him not to go, weeping, pulling at him.

He kept pushing me off, weeping too, saying he couldn't stay any longer.

I wept and screamed for him to stay.

He relented and we hugged. I brought him back in.

I was so happy to see him back (and did not consider the implications of staying together for them.)

I no longer hated him as an abuser, I loved him as a man who did many wonderful things for me. I loved him for the bright, interesting man that he was. I thanked him for life.

April 1

All Fools Day.

I saw my brother today. He will read this one day and know what a fool he's been. When I said: who are you? He replied: I am the child of your father and mother. What sort of answer is that?

I was amazed at how he had changed, of course. It also dawned on me instantly that I could have expected nothing else. The surprise was in seeing him, not in his having aged.

His nature made me feel good inside, warm and touched. I laughed, too, from my belly. He really did feel like my special brother.I like the way he laughs.

April 10

The first three body weights are like silver-white globes, one on top of the other. On top of the smallest one there is an even smaller ball that is somehow transparent but it glows at the same time. It hovers just above the other three. It looks heavy with energy, like it could zap things. All these four globes are contained in a larger globe that looks like a very thinly stretched see-through balloon. It vibrates slowly, like it is filled with water. It makes me feel dizzy.

Hold the fourth weight balanced on top of the other three, focus there, hold it – stop. That's it, now the balloon stops swaying - and you can step into it. Just step forward.

I opened my eyes and looked around me.

I can walk in the garden again, only this time I notice where I am and can find the centre.

April 13

I embrace the chalice and drink of the well of life. I choose to awaken.

Make a mudra shape: faith is wings.

Existent for millions of years, I create myself in each moment of time: Knowledge (points) items, Understanding (a line) connection, Wisdom (triangle) perspective/meaning, Application (solid) making solid. This is my life now: I am the flow of willing and this I create.

I am a being of no particular size or shape
And I inhabit this beautiful body.

June 30

Tonight's the night. There will be no dawn tomorrow for me. Only my own dawn, golden dawn, glittering stars…

Sage flowers, on rich, thick purple spikes of flowers, reaching to the light, to the setting sun, their mouths open crying out for pollination. They grow in a clump at the edge of the path, their purple light dazzling the setting sun. Swain wind, roughly, done, they sway in the wind, gently, confidently. Insects buzz in their aura, particularly large bees, golden brown bodies hovering at the flowers' mouths. I lean forward, my head entering the intoxicating auric field of the plants. Scent is sweet and overwhelms. I am captivated in an extended moment, totally present and at the same time conscious of every other time I have related to my Sage, my sweet Angel.

July 1

Late at night almost midnight – here we go:

Each cloud has a face, a constantly evolving visage that reflects back to the looker the state of his or her own consciousness at that time. So you might see a crying girl – what are you crying about? Or you see a great god figure and you ask yourself who am I? Or you see an archetypal scene and are shown therein an archetypal pattern of your own life.

Just as clouds have faces, so faces have clouds. Ask yourself, who is this person I am looking at? Who am I? When you get the answer, don't go into the answer but come from it, back into the place where your question originated. Come back with the answer and hold your new awareness. It's not where you are going to that matters, it is where you are coming from.

July 22

Here I am, standing on earth again. Today. Here. When the water and air and fire are balanced, the earth and the spirit are united.

At this precise moment, a yellow dragonfly lands to my left, its strangely alien and enticingly beautiful body shimmering in the setting sun. In each of its million eyes I see an image of myself at the centre of the sphere of the garden.

July 23

Another glorious day as I sit and write this in the shade of a large copper beech tree in this beautiful garden. My journal is like my body with its sun-bleached cover and the blood in its veins. I'm an unfolding book, another page turns, and turns, and turns yet in this moment, I am all that I can be.

Love is the great circle of time, will is what turns the wheel and imagination is what brings it to life.